KONA BREEZE

Darcy Rice

ZEBRA BOOKS
KENSINGTON PUBLISHING CORP.

For all our new friends we found
on the Big Island, and for all our
old friends who found us there.

ZEBRA BOOKS are published by

Kensington Publishing Corp.
850 Third Avenue
New York, NY 10022

First Zebra Printing: May, 1996
10 9 8 7 6 5 4 3 2 1

Printed in the United States of America

One

"Damn it to hell!"

The big yellow dog in the corner, startled awake by the sound of breaking glass and her master's angry voice, lifted her head and looked at the man with concern. Cord Barrett's sharp blue eyes met the dog's soft brown ones. He stopped short in mid-curse and exhaled slowly, suddenly embarrassed by his outburst. He took a silent moment and willed himself to let his anger and frustration go. It was only a glass of orange juice, after all.

"Sorry, Scuba. Didn't mean to disturb you. Glass was a little slippery, that's all." The dog snorted her gracious acceptance of Cord's apology and put her head back down on her paws to return to her morning nap. "That's right, girl. Get back to your beauty sleep."

Although Cord had lived alone for years, he had never been a man who talked to himself. But to his chagrin, just lately he'd caught himself talking out loud to Scuba about all kinds of things, jabbering on like some crazy *luahine* to her houseful of cats. Harmless enough, but for some reason he couldn't put his finger on, the habit irritated the hell out of him. Probably he was just getting a touch of cabin fever, that was all. On top of everything else.

After all, Cord knew what was really wrong with him. There was no mystery about it. He was sick of fighting these damn crutches, that was the problem. Even making breakfast was a major production—but of course everything in his life seemed to be like that now, ever since the accident. Breakfast was hardly something worth getting upset over. And besides, he had far bigger problems to worry about right now.

Cord stared down at the scarred linoleum where a pulpy orange puddle was spreading over the floor and the shards of glass. He'd better get this mess cleaned up. He grabbed the broom, and with his elbows locked tight against his body to hold the crutches steady, he swept the glass into a wet pile in the middle of the floor. Supported by the crutches, he balanced on his good left leg to keep his plaster-encased right leg elevated off the floor and out of the sticky mess.

A trickle of sweat began to drip down his temple. The muscles in his hip and thigh were trembling with the effort of keeping the leg up, but he gritted his teeth and finished sweeping before he leaned back against the counter to rest. He took a couple of deep breaths and wiped the sweat off his face with the bottom of his T-shirt. "I don't know how you can sleep in this heat, dog," he muttered into the damp fabric as he scrubbed his face.

Although it was only a few minutes past eight, the air in the tiny house was already warm and dense with humidity. After fifteen years on the Big Island of Hawaii, Cord still found these muggy June days a bit oppressive; but he usually considered those few weeks a small price to pay for living in paradise the rest of the year.

But this June it seemed far worse than it ever had in previous years. He couldn't say for certain whether that was due to his rotten attitude, or simply due to the hot and sticky weather that was making the skin underneath his cast itch like crazy. All he knew was that he was as uncomfortable as hell.

Cord looked with disgust from the ragged pile of glass on the floor to his right leg. The once-white plaster cast, now grimy from three weeks of wear, ran from the middle of his foot all the way up his leg, disappearing into his baggy shorts where it ended only a few inches short of his groin. Getting down on the floor and back up again would be a bitch of a problem, but he had to get the broken glass cleaned up. It was too dangerous for Scuba if he were to leave it there, or even sweep it into a corner. She could end up with a piece lodged in her nose or her paw, and he was in no condition to take her to the vet or to even doctor her himself.

Cord found the dustpan and dampened a dish towel with water. He carefully laid his crutches aside as he wedged his back firmly against the pantry cupboard door. He began a slow slide down, keeping his back tight against the smooth wood as he gingerly lowered himself, his left leg bearing his weight in a crouch as his plaster-encased right leg splayed out stiffly in front of him.

The rest of his body, still bruised and tender, was beginning to throb with discomfort. It seemed to take forever for him to reach the floor; then finally he was there. He caught his breath for a few minutes, then began the awkward task of cleaning up the shards of glass and spilled juice.

Soon Cord had both the big pieces and the tiny splinters of glass collected in the plastic dustpan and the orange juice wiped up. He scanned the floor carefully for any more missing fragments and found two tiny ones. Finally, he passed his hand over the floor slowly, before he was satisfied that he had found all the broken glass.

He remained sitting on the floor without moving as he tried to figure out the easiest way to get back up. In the middle of considering his options, suddenly the absurdity of the situation struck him, and he emitted a short, humorless bark of laughter. The situation was beyond absurd; it was pathetic.

Only a very short time ago, not even a month ago, his life had been entirely different. But now that life seemed so far away, almost like a fast-fading dream or some kind of childhood fantasy.

By this time of the morning he would almost always be found in the same place: the cockpit of his helicopter. By now, he would have already finished his opening safety speech to his first passengers of the day, seated them according to correct weight distribution, made certain they were all securely belted in, and taken his position in the cockpit.

Cord leaned his head back against the cabinet and closed his eyes, letting himself give in to the seductive memory, and suddenly, he was there once again, flying high over the rugged lava fields and lush rain forests of the Big Island. Even in memory, the power and the freedom of flight were like some supernatural force that he could feel through to the very core of his body.

But that wasn't reality. Not anymore. His eyes snapped open. Reality was him sitting here in the middle of his kitchen floor on a sticky June morning, sweating like a dog with the simple effort of getting up and down.

But no matter what, he was a lucky man, and he must not forget it. Even the doctors who had set his broken leg—careful, scientific men who were not given to overstatement—even those men had called his condition a miracle. Cord had never been much for believing in miracles, but in this case he knew they were telling the truth. By all rights, he should be dead. Simply surviving a small-aircraft accident was far more than any pilot had a right to expect.

Three weeks ago he'd been flying alone, on his way back from taking a routine charter from the Kona side of the island to the airport in Hilo, when a freak storm swept down the western slope of Mauna Kea and forced his helicopter down with shattering force; like an enormous hand crushing an insect.

Several hours later, when he regained partial consciousness, he was in the trauma center surrounded by efficient doctors and nurses. Their pale green scrubs were daubed with vivid splotches that, through his dimly flickering awareness, he had slowly come to realize were splashes of his own blood. As he grappled with that discovery, a new needle pierced his arm, and he lost consciousness in a swirl of pain and anesthesia. He did not reawaken for nearly two days.

After his emergency surgery, Cord stayed in the hospital for less than a week, insisting all the while that he would rather recover at home. The doctors were reluctant at first, but he raised so much hell they finally consented, with the condition that twice-weekly follow-up visits be made by one of the three traveling nurses who served the most remote areas of the Big Island.

He'd been home now for two weeks. His leg was broken in three places, but they were all nice clean breaks. The golf ball-sized knot on his head had almost disappeared, although the slightly raised spot where it had been still hurt like hell when he put a finger to it. And although his torso was still purple with bruises in several places, he'd suffered no serious internal injuries. He was still quite sore, and would be for a while, the doctors had assured him of that. The cast on his leg would stay on for another couple of months, and even once it was off, he'd still need several additional months of therapy to regain full use of his leg. But as the doctors kept reminding him, he was one incredibly lucky guy.

Lucky. Right. Unfortunately, if things didn't change soon, it looked as though his luck was about to run out. His helicopter tour and charter business, Big Island Wings, had provided him a decent living for years. Okay, to be completely honest, it'd been barely profitable some of those years, but he still had enough money to live the way he wanted, in the place he wanted. Most important of all to Cord, he was making a living flying his helicopter and he didn't have to answer to anyone. He was his own boss.

He was accountable to no one but himself. It was his choice to work or to spend the day at the beach. Nobody was looking over his shoulder, just as nobody cared what he ate for dinner or what time he went to bed or got up in the morning. He did exactly as he pleased.

Sure, he was lonely sometimes. He was used to that. But a little loneliness was nothing compared to the pain that came with getting all tied up in somebody else's life. He knew all too well what that was like, and he wouldn't let it happen again. He wasn't that stupid.

But everything about his life was going to change very soon if he didn't figure a way out of the mess he'd gotten himself into. The repairs to his aircraft would be paid for by insurance, but the huge deductible had completely wiped out what meager savings he had. In fact, although the repairs had been completed for over a week, the bird was still sitting over at the repair yard because he was still several thousand dollars short of meeting the deductible.

Getting his copter back was really the least of his problems, since he couldn't fly with his leg in a cast anyway. As much as he hated to admit it even to himself, he was grounded for the next two months. No amount of willpower could change that. And without some kind of drastic action, he would be financially destroyed well before that. Everything he'd ever given a damn about would be taken from him. Everything. The thought had settled into his stomach like some hard, undigested lump.

Cord shifted position on the cool linoleum and glanced at the clock on the wall. 8:25. The traveling nurse from the hospital would be here very soon to check on his progress. He wondered which one it would be this time: the older, motherly one with the salt-and-pepper hair who loved to laugh and talk or the younger one with the bleached-blond hair and thick glasses. Although the women were always kind and efficient as they went about their work, Cord guessed that both of them considered him a rather difficult patient. He could sense that, in spite of their professional manners.

Hell, he probably *was* difficult, and being poked and prodded sure didn't do anything to improve his admittedly surly disposition. Well, no matter which one of them showed up this time, he didn't want her to find him sprawled on the floor like a drunk. With a report like that, the doctors would order him back to the hospital for sure, and there was no way he was going back there. Gritting his teeth, he braced himself for the pain of getting back up.

He used one of his crutches for support as he struggled to his feet. He leaned against the counter, catching his breath, when he heard the car drive up outside. Scuba jumped up, barking fiercely. "It's okay, girl, it's okay. Calm down. Just one of our regular visitors, nothing to get excited about." Cord positioned his crutches under his arms and made his way to the door.

Randee Turner slammed the mud-spattered door of her van and took a long look at the strange structure in front of her. The dirt road she had followed down the hillside for the past half-mile after turning off the highway came to a dead end here, so this had to be the right place, but she still searched for some sign to reassure her.

Dense coffee bushes surrounded a small clearing on the hillside, from which she could see the blue water of the Pacific far below. In the middle of the clearing stood a small wooden shack with a ramshackle lanai on the ocean side. An old Jeep was parked next to the shack, only half covered by a dirty canvas tarp.

Randee took the whole scene in, comparing what she saw with what she knew of the man who lived there, trying to make sense of two wildly divergent images. She hadn't been entirely sure what to expect, but this certainly wasn't it. This place looked like the retreat of some of the counterculture types left over from the sixties who still lived on the island. But Randee knew it was the home of the man widely reputed to be the best helicopter pilot in Hawaii.

Randee clutched her leather case under her arm and took a deep breath. The surprise aspect of her visit made her nervous, but she hadn't had any choice about that. Apparently the mysterious Mr. Barrett disliked telephones as much as he did neighbors, and Randee wasn't willing to wait for the mail. She didn't have that much time, and she wasn't willing to take the chance of being denied a face-to-face meeting. That was why, she reminded herself, dropping in unannounced was probably for the best. A proposition like hers really had to be discussed in person.

Besides, this was not a time for timidity. This wasn't just for her. Much more was at stake today. Rorey was counting on her. As Randee thought of him, a surge of fierce love steeled her resolve to get what she'd come for. She would not let him down. She let that thought overcome her trepidation and propel her forward.

Randee picked her way around the puddles left from last night's rain, now steaming in the morning sun, and up the three steps that led to the lanai and the only door. She scrubbed the bottoms of her best shoes against the rough woven mat, hoping to get rid of the mud that was clinging to them, as she searched for some kind of doorbell. Finding none, she raised her fist to knock.

Before her knuckles had even made contact with the wood, the door flew open. A tall man now filled the space where the door had been, his lanky frame supported by crutches. A large yellow dog was at his side, friendly-looking, but watching her closely.

"At least you're on time today." Bright blue eyes focused on her briefly, registering surprise, as if he'd been expecting someone else. "Oh, sorry. I thought you were, what's-her-name, Marge. She's usually late."

The man stepped back, moving quickly in spite of the plaster cast that covered his entire right leg. "It's not that I have any pressing engagements to attend to or anything like that. Can't do anything with this damn thing on my leg. But for what it's worth, I still hate to wait." He gestured impatiently with one crutch. "Well, come on in. Let's get this over with. Go lay down, Scuba. Lay down, girl. Let the lady do her job." The dog trotted obediently to her bed in the corner but still remained watchful.

The man moved to the center of the cluttered room, which seemed to serve as both bedroom and living room. "I sure hope you brought me something for the itching. It's driving me crazy. I told Marge last week that I'm about ready to take a hacksaw

and cut this stupid thing right off my leg. I don't know how long
I'm going to last."

Randee followed him into the small room, her carefully planned
and rehearsed introduction forgotten, as she tried to evaluate what
was happening in front of her. Several people had described Cord
Barrett to her; a big man, tall, they'd said, and good-looking, in
a rough kind of way. But those pallid descriptions had done nothing to prepare her for meeting the man in the flesh.

Cord Barrett *was* tall, at least several inches over six feet, and
even on crutches he was an imposing figure. His hair was an
unruly mass of dark, shaggy blond threaded with a few streaks
of gray, like the mane of a lion. His face was too strongly featured
to be considered traditionally handsome—high cheekbones, strong
nose, square jaw—a series of hard planes that were softened only
by a full, sensual mouth. His eyes were an intense shade of blue
framed by thick blond lashes bleached nearly white at the tips.

Cord leaned his crutches against the back of the worn corduroy
sofa that was one of the only pieces of furniture in the room, and
balanced for a moment on his good leg. To Randee's astonishment,
he stripped his T-shirt off over his head in a single graceful, efficient motion and tossed it carelessly over the back of the couch.
Her mouth went suddenly dry.

Cord's torso was leanly muscled, broad shoulders tapering to a
narrow waist. His skin was a tawny golden color and smooth,
with only a light dusting of coppery curls that covered his chest
across the broadest point, and arrowed down his flat stomach to
disappear beneath the waistband of the well-worn cotton shorts
that rode low on his hips. Only a few fading bruises marred the
solid perfection of his body.

Examining his body with a detached, critical eye, like some
troublesome piece of machinery, one that wasn't performing up
to his standards, Cord touched the largest and darkest of the
bruises, which started below his ribs on his left side and extended
down toward his hip.

"Most of the purple's finally gone, I think, except for down
here." He hooked a thumb into the elastic waistband of his shorts
and casually peeled it down several inches below his hip, exposing
both the rest of the bruise as well as the clearly delineated line

between his deeply tanned torso and the lighter skin of his hip and lower abdomen. "See, this is the only really bad spot left—"

"Mr. Barrett." Randee's voice came out in a dry croak, as though she needed a drink of water. Cord Barrett's strange house suddenly seemed very, very remote. No telephone. No neighbors. What had she gotten herself into? She remembered the twisting dirt road that had brought her here; she'd passed no other buildings.

Although he'd said nothing menacing, had made no move toward her, Randee felt tremendously vulnerable. He was a man who was capable of taking exactly what he wanted, when he wanted. His hard body and his self-assured attitude made that absolutely clear. Involuntarily, her eyes returned to his work-corded forearms and his large, rough hands. She found herself imagining the strength of those hands.

She wet her lips with her tongue and searched for words. Her heart was pounding, but she took a deep breath and managed to keep her voice steady.

"Mr. Barrett, I'm afraid there's been some confusion. Let me introduce myself; my name is Randee Turner. I'm terribly sorry, but I think—no, I am absolutely *sure* that you have mistaken me for someone else, I don't know who. But I am here to talk business."

When Cord Barrett didn't respond, she took another deliberately slow breath and tried to look away, to avert her eyes from his nearly naked body standing with solid defiance in front of her, but in spite of her efforts, her eyes remained fixed on him.

Unnerved by his silence, Randee forced herself to plunge ahead, desperately trying to regain control of this situation. "Please don't take offense, but I would really prefer for you to get dressed before we begin."

Confused and annoyed, Cord pulled his shorts back up over his hip. For the first time since she'd arrived at his door, he took a good look at the petite woman in front of him. She certainly didn't have the no-nonsense look that the other two nurses did; no white coat, and no name badge, either. As he let his gaze wander slowly over her, Cord realized he had made a mistake, a big mistake.

The woman's hair was a dark mane of chestnut, piled up on

her head in what looked like an attempt at sophisticated restraint, but soft tendrils had escaped and fallen over the graceful column of her neck and framed her delicate features. Her face was flushed with color. Deep green eyes, tiny nose dusted with a few freckles, and a full, luscious mouth. An impudent mouth, one that seemed to challenge a man to take it with his own.

She was wearing a silky dress of jade green, too dressy for this rural area of Hawaii, especially in this sticky heat, but that exactly matched the astonishing color of her eyes and was short enough to show off a pair of long, shapely legs. The neckline was discreet but still managed to give just a hint of full, lush cleavage beneath the shimmering fabric. A woman's shape.

This woman practically exuded money and class. She was sexy as hell, no doubt about that, but she was about as out of place in his converted coffee shack as a visitor from Venus. So what was she doing here?

"What exactly do you mean, 'talk business'?" Cord picked up the T-shirt but didn't bother putting it back on. After all, he hadn't asked this woman to come out here, and besides, it felt as if the air in the room was getting steamier by the second. Cord wiped a trickle of sweat from his forehead with the T-shirt, waiting for her to answer his question, challenging her to explain.

Seemingly unaffected by the heat, the woman looked as fresh as if she'd just stepped out of a perfectly air-conditioned penthouse. She seemed in no hurry to speak. When she didn't answer and he could no longer tolerate the silence, he tried again.

"So what do you want? Why are you here?"

She paused and took a deep breath before she answered, and Cord could see the rise and fall of her full breasts beneath the green silk, and he suddenly imagined the cool feel of that silk sliding beneath his searching fingers.

"I am here, Mr. Barrett, because I am going to help you save Big Island Wings."

Two

"Save my business? What the hell are you talking about?" Cord's curiosity was transformed into suspicion. "What's going on here?"

"Nothing mysterious, I can assure you. I simply saw your ad in the newspaper, Mr. Barrett, and I made some inquiries about you, became familiar with your situation. I am convinced that we can work something out."

The proud lift of the woman's chin and her cool voice unreasonably irritated him, but Cord tried not to let his feelings show. He'd placed the ad she was talking about more than two weeks ago, when he finally admitted to himself that he was going to lose his business if he didn't take some kind of drastic action.

Although he told himself over and over that he was only doing what he had to do, only doing what was absolutely necessary with the crappy hand life had recently dealt him, even so, the first time he had actually seen the ad in print under the "Business Opportunities" section of the classified ads he felt as if he were going to be sick. The carefully chosen words seemed to mock him, to underscore his helplessness.

Established business seeking silent partner with capital to contribute to solve temporary cash flow problems. Excellent opportunity for absentee investor. Direct inquiries to Cord Barrett, Big Island Wings, P.O. Box 243, Honaunau, HI 97245.

In the time since he placed the ad, his misery had only deepened. The ad had been running for two weeks, and he had not received even one response, nothing, not even a curious inquiry or a crackpot offer. The only things he'd found in his P.O. box lately were bills, all of them past due. There was no doubt about it, he was in a tough spot, and somehow this seductive stranger seemed to know it. Cord scrutinized the woman in green silk again.

"Look, Miss, ah—"

"Randee Turner." Cord noticed that as she spoke, she pulled the leather case she carried a bit tighter to her body. It was an almost nervous gesture that struck him as out of place, an odd contrast to her sophisticated, polished appearance and controlled manner of speaking. Perhaps the lady wasn't quite as cool as she first appeared.

"So Miss Randee Turner, what exactly are you trying to get at here?"

"First of all, you haven't made any other arrangements yet, have you?"

Now the tentative moment had passed, and with that question, she was back in control. Any uncertainty he'd thought he'd seen in her had now vanished. The tone of her voice and the arch of her eyebrows implied that she knew full well that he hadn't had so much as a nibble of interest, but that she wouldn't embarrass him by saying so directly. In fact, she asked the question as if she knew a lot of other things about him as well.

The thought made him damn uncomfortable. His mind raced backward through the conversation. What the hell did she mean when she said she'd "made some inquiries"? He didn't like the sound of that.

"Mr. Barrett?"

"No. No, I haven't accepted another offer, if that's what you mean. Not yet." Like hell. Like he'd received *any* offers. This woman certainly didn't look like his idea of a silent partner in a helicopter business. She looked like—he wasn't exactly sure, not yet, but suddenly he felt her eyes on his body and he became aware that he was still naked to the waist, holding his crumpled T-shirt in his hand.

Cord felt uncomfortably exposed, and at a distinct disadvantage. He quickly pulled the shirt on over his head and replaced his crutches under his arms. The air was growing thicker, and his leg was starting to throb. He needed to move around a bit.

He crossed to the other side of the room and fiddled with the broad plantation shutters that took the place of glass in the window, opening them as wide as they would go, hoping for even the smallest puff of breeze to relieve the sweltering heat, but nothing stirred.

"So what does that have to do with you?"

"We are in similar businesses, Mr. Barrett."

"We are?" His voice was heavy with sarcasm. "I find that hard to believe."

If the woman noticed his rudeness, she was choosing to ignore it. She didn't lose her own businesslike tone. "Do you know the *Kona Breeze?*"

Cord nodded, impatient. Of course he recognized the *Kona Breeze*. The big trimaran was an institution on the Kona coast. The boat had been taking tourists down the coast to the protected marine reserve of Kealakekua Bay for snorkeling and scuba diving ever since he'd been on the Big Island, and probably for long before that.

"So you work for Jack Haster?" That seemed extremely unlikely. Cord had met Haster several times a number of years ago, and he'd been a crusty old salt with a quick temper and a sailor's mouth. Cord couldn't imagine him putting up with a hothouse flower like this lady anywhere around his operation, not for five minutes, in spite of her looks.

"No, I don't work for Haster. I am now the owner of the *Kona Breeze.*"

"You own that boat? Since when?" His obvious disbelief made the question a rude challenge, but Randee Turner appeared unruffled.

"I acquired it only a few months ago, but believe me, I'm learning fast." She smiled, now gently self-deprecating. "And I'll admit there's been a lot to learn. And a lot of damage to repair."

Cord narrowed his eyes in skepticism. There was no way in God's wide world that this woman had anything to do with a big working boat like the *Kona Breeze*. She looked like one of the wealthy tourists who frequented the upscale resorts of the Kohala coast, one of the beautiful, pampered women who divided their time between shopping in the expensive boutiques in the hotels and baking themselves to perfection on the beach. He'd seen untold numbers of such women in his time on Hawaii, flown quite a few of them in his copter as well; that is, when their indulgent husbands could drag them away from shopping for a couple of hours.

"What do you mean by damage?"

"Jack Haster's health wasn't good the last few years, and as a result the business had been allowed to go downhill, but that's changed now that I'm there. My goal is to increase the boat's passenger load a minimum of fifty percent by the end of this year."

Cord was confused. The woman was beginning to sound like she knew what she was talking about. Could it possibly be true? He had to admit it, there was nothing about her that suggested she was a liar—or crazy. In fact, her calm assurance gave her an air of considerable credibility. Still, it was hard to believe. His mind searched for another explanation, but found none.

Okay, so maybe she did own the *Kona Breeze*. Maybe a rich husband had bought it for her as a plaything, a little something to keep his sexy wife occupied. Probably more fun than bossing around the servants. She could play at her little business and toss it aside when she tired of the game. He looked at her hands, long, graceful fingers, perfect nails; she'd probably never done a day of real work in her life.

"So what do you and the *Kona Breeze* have to do with me and my business?"

"Everything, Mr. Barrett. I'm here to make a deal with you. I know that you are looking for a partner to contribute the capital you need to stay in business until you recover. I would like to be that partner."

"So why didn't you just answer my ad?"

"I felt that it was best for us to meet face-to-face, Mr. Barrett, so that we might talk terms. I've got a lot of resources to offer you. As you know, we must act quickly. I believe that I can help you not only save your company from disaster, but make it much more profitable in the future as well."

"I see."

Cord felt blood rushing to his face. Who the hell did this

woman think she was, anyway? He'd been flying these islands for fifteen years, and now she was going to "save him from disaster," as she put it? He recognized her type. Rich, bored, and looking for another little project to keep busy. Just the kind of woman who'd get her kicks out of playing Lady Bountiful to a gimpy copter pilot living in a converted coffee shack. Well, she could find some other poor bastard, he wasn't playing along.

Cord crossed the short distance to the door, a faint sweet fragrance teasing his senses as he passed close to her, and his body tightened in response. Fighting his body's unwelcome reaction, he opened the door and gestured pointedly with one crutch.

"I'm not interested." He wanted her out, and fast. The effect she was having on him physically only served to heighten his anger at her presence.

"But—"

"This conversation is over." The sooner she was out of here, the better off he would be. She was screwing up his thinking.

The woman hesitated for a moment, as if considering her response, then, silently, she walked to the door. She stopped short of the doorway and turned back, her body only a few inches from his. As she confronted him, she looked up into his eyes without flinching.

"You're being extremely unreasonable, Mr. Barrett." Her voice was polite, but Cord sensed an undercurrent of steel that grabbed his attention. "At the risk of offending you even further, I might even say you're being foolish." Her vivid green eyes searched his face. "You haven't even heard my offer. You need someone right away, whether you want to admit it or not, I know that."

Cord concentrated on keeping emotion out of his face, but he felt she was seeing through him anyway. He didn't trust himself to answer.

"I think you owe it to yourself to hear me out. You're in quite a fix, Mr. Barrett. You know it and I know it. You won't be able to stay afloat much longer."

Anger ripped through his gut like a knife. An obscenity leapt to his lips, but he bit it back before he spoke it aloud. She was right. Damn it, the woman was right. Two weeks, and not another prospect in sight. Just Randee Turner of the sexy legs and luscious mouth and infuriating attitude. As of this moment, she was all that was standing between him and bankruptcy. But bankruptcy or not, it still took every ounce of discipline Cord possessed to resist the impulse to give her a good shove out the door.

"All right, I'll listen. Make it quick. What's your offer?" He kept her eyes locked onto his. He wouldn't make this easy for her.

"Don't you need to sit down, Mr. Barrett? I mean your leg must be—"

"My leg's just fine. Get to the point. So what's your offer?"

Randee moistened her lips, the details of her well-rehearsed speech swimming in her head, a useless muddle of detail. She mustn't let her desperation show. Too much was at stake in this little poker game they were playing. She thought again of Rorey, and her head cleared.

"You've had some bad luck, Mr. Barrett."

Cord grunted, a low sound of mixed disgust and acknowledgment. He shrugged his massive shoulders. "Sure. I guess you could call it that. But not near as bad as it could have been. So why don't you just leave my luck out of it and get to the point?"

Randee suddenly was overwhelmed by the realization that she was very close, much too close to this man, boxed in between the doorway and his solid body. She carefully walked to the coffee table and put down her small briefcase, glad for any excuse to put a little distance between herself and Cord Barrett. Her legs felt shaky beneath her.

When she turned back, his face had been transformed into an indifferent mask that betrayed no feeling. For some reason that was even more unnerving than his earlier overt hostility. Randee took refuge in the words she'd practiced a dozen times out loud at home.

"This is what I propose. The most important thing is to get your helicopter back in the air. Not only are you not making any money, but each day that goes by without a flight puts a dent in the substantial market share that Big Island Wings has carved out over the last few years."

His expression remained indifferent. She took a breath and rushed on ahead, half expecting him to interrupt her at any moment. "You've got an excellent reputation, I've talked to enough people to know that, and I know that most of your business has come by word of mouth. But now that you're not flying, other operators are taking advantage of your unfortunate predicament, picking up the customers that should have been yours."

Randee waited for some acknowledgment that he was following her line of thinking, but his face was still impassive as stone. She cleared her throat and continued. "So, as I said earlier, I've made some inquiries about your situation. I understand that the aircraft has been repaired but is still being held at the yard?"

"That's right."

"I assume that is because you don't have the funds to pay the deductible?"

The tiniest flicker of annoyance passed over Cord's face, then disappeared.

"You assume right."

"I will pay the balance still due on the bill. I will also pay the salary of a replacement pilot while you are recovering. With some work and a little luck, we could be flying again by next week."

"We could, could we?" Cord's voice was even, but ragged, as if he were holding his emotions carefully in check.

"Yes, that's right. Now there's also the premium on your liability insurance, which is—"

"Past due." Cord's eyes flashed. "But I'm sure you already knew that."

"Well, I have—"

"Made some inquiries. Right. Go on."

"I will pay the premium now due so we'll be legal to fly." Randee paused, trying to read the situation, but she couldn't be sure how she was doing. The man was proud, that was for certain, maybe too proud for his own good. She cleared her throat again and forced herself to plunge ahead. "And then there's the matter of your draw." Randee waited for him to respond, but Cord remained silent. "I mean, of course I understand that you have to be able to live."

Cord's mouth twisted in a grim approximation of a smile. "Yes, I suppose you could say that."

"I will pay you whatever amount you have been accustomed to taking out of the business, until you are fully recovered and able to fly again."

"And what do you expect in return for all your generosity in my time of need?"

A long moment stretched between them like a deep chasm.

"You will give me fifty-one percent ownership in Big Island Wings."

The big man looked as if he'd been kicked in the stomach. Randee waited for him to speak, a long, silent minute. She expected an explosion, but when he finally did speak, his voice was frighteningly low.

"So what's this all about, really? What's in it for you? Have you just always had some strange, overwhelming desire to own a helicopter business?"

"No, that's not it, not exactly." Randee's heart was pounding. She had expected a strong reaction, but nothing had prepared her for this. She could feel the palpable force of his anger underscoring each word.

"But I'll bet you always get what you want, don't you? Whatever money can buy." His voice was controlled, but it dripped with disdain. Cord turned and walked out the door, his crutches striking the wooden floor with a hollow sound.

Randee waited inside for a long minute, considering, unable to move. She couldn't fail now. She could not let it end like this. She chose her course of action and followed him out the door.

Outside, Cord stood at the railing of the small, rustic lanai that stretched from end to end of the house. He was looking out toward the dense coffee groves that covered the hillsides, and far below at the blue water of the Pacific.

"Look, Mr. Barrett." Randee addressed his broad back. She couldn't see his face. "I know how hard this must be for you. I'm truly sorry about your accident. But this is a business proposition, and it's designed to be mutually beneficial. If any partnership is going to work, that's the way it has to be." She studied his back for a sign that he was listening, but found none.

"You need me, that's true. But Big Island Wings is a good investment for me, as well." Randee edged forward to the railing, but was careful not to look in Cord's direction. *Be careful,* she reminded herself, *don't let him know how much you need him.*

Randee took a deep breath and continued. "As I told you earlier, I need to increase business on the *Kona Breeze.* But as I'm sure you know, there's a lot of competition. A visitor can just as easily go out on the *Captain Cook,* or the *Parry Boat,* or any of the other smaller operations. But if I package trips on my boat with your helicopter tours and price them aggressively, I can sell that combination to the big tour operators, especially the ones that cater to the Japanese tourists. It'll open up a whole new market for both of us. And that's a whole new source of business, business that neither one of us is getting right now."

She chanced a look at Cord's face, but she couldn't read his response. "If things go well, we could add another helicopter and pilot by next year."

Randee waited for some indication of Cord's feelings, but none came. "So, to answer your earlier question, Mr. Barrett, what's in it for me, as you put it, is simply a very good investment. And I believe that's exactly what it will be for you as well."

For the first time since moving outside, Cord spoke.

"And why fifty-one percent?" Even in the sticky summer morning, his words were icy.

"I must have control of all my investments, Mr. Barrett. That's my policy." *Policy,* she thought wryly. *I suppose that's one way of putting it.* The simple fact was that she would never again make the mistake of letting a man have power over her. That was a lesson she had learned the hard way, and she wasn't ever going to forget it. Not only for her own sake, but for Rorey's as well. She had to protect both of them. They were on their own now. Randee held her breath, waiting for Cord's response.

Cord considered kicking Randee Turner's sexy little butt right off his lanai. He considered telling her to get the hell off his property. He considered telling her exactly what he thought of her little proposition, with the kind of descriptive language he hadn't used since he was discharged from the Marine Corps sixteen years ago.

But he didn't do any of those things. With a sudden terrible certainty, he realized he didn't have a choice. Randee Turner's offer was his only hope of keeping his copter, his business, his house—really, everything he cared about in his life—from being swept away in a sea of red ink. He forced himself to speak.

"Okay."

"Okay?" Her tone told him she expected more.

"I mean, I accept your offer." The words stuck in his throat like stale bread. "But if I do, then there's got to be one additional condition."

"Name it."

"I want the right to buy back your fifty-one percent at any time."

"At a fair market value that I will determine at that time?" Her eyes flashed emerald fire.

"Yes. At whatever value you determine." Cord felt the hopelessness of his demand even as he spoke it. It was a pointless gesture. He'd never be able to get control of his business back, never.

"In that case, Mr. Barrett, I think we have a deal."

Three

Randee turned the key in the lock and slowly opened the door. She tiptoed in and closed it behind her. As she turned around, a short, stocky Hawaiian woman emerged from the hall, a stubby finger pressed to her lips.

"Shh, the *keiki* is asleep."

At the reassuring sight of the older woman's broad, peaceful face, framed by a river of thick dark hair, Randee felt some of the morning's tension melt from her body and a smile rise unbidden to her lips.

"Of course. Rorey never fights nap time when his Auntie Lani is taking care of him. I only wish I knew your secret." She put her briefcase down on the kitchen table. "I'll go take a peek at him."

Randee slipped into the tiny bedroom where Rorey slept peacefully in his crib. She stood by the edge of his crib for several minutes, watching him sleep, overcome with love. The sheer wonder of his existence still had the power to overwhelm her.

As she had done countless times since he was born, Randee marveled at the subtle changes that she saw in her son each day. Now, at eighteen months old, Rorey often seemed much closer to being a little boy than a baby. But at times like this, when he was wrapped in the silent innocence of sleep, Randee could still see him as the tiny, helpless infant she had brought into the world.

The last two years had passed so quickly. Much of that time had been filled with anger and pain and sorrow, floods of hurtful and destructive emotions, but nothing could destroy her joy over Rorey.

Nothing in this world had that power. In spite of all that had happened, she would never regret this miracle. All the hell she'd been through couldn't take that happiness from her. That belonged to her alone.

She reached out and stroked Rorey's cheek with one finger. His skin was smooth and warm to her touch. He stirred in his sleep, tiny perfect lips murmuring some secret of his baby dreams. Randee felt her eyes moisten. She rubbed the tears away before she quietly slipped from the room.

Lani was waiting at the door, her oversized straw handbag on her arm. She paused with her hand on the knob and carefully assessed Randee with her dark, sparkling eyes, sharp eyes that missed very little. "So, did everything go okay today with your Mr. Barrett?"

"Fine, just fine."

"You sure about that?"

Randee smiled and gave her a quick hug. "Yes, I'm sure, Lani. Now don't *you* start worrying. Everything's going to be great."

Lani gave a small skeptical nod. "Okay, if you say so. I'm not going to pry. But Auntie Lani's not blind, you know. I see what I see. You look a little *ma'i* to me."

"I'm not sick, Lani, honest. Just a little worn out."

"Hmm. If you say so. Then you better put your feet up and rest for a few minutes. There's a pot of fresh coffee in the kitchen."

"You're an angel."

"Take good care of my *keiki*. Call me if you need me. I'm only next door, you know." Lani slipped out the door. "See you later."

Randee smiled at Lani's broad back disappearing through the door. She was so grateful to have her close by. Fate had brought them together at a time when Randee desperately needed someone to help her look after Rorey. The day Randee and Rorey moved in, Lani had arrived at their door with fresh-baked cookies to welcome them to their new home. Lani lived in the small apartment attached to the main house. This type of apartment, or *ohana,* as it was known, was a common feature of many homes in Hawaii, and many families had a grandmother or aunt who lived in such cozy quarters.

Rorey had instantly bonded with the motherly woman, and Randee knew that her search for a special person to take care of

Rorey was over. It wasn't long before she came to think of Lani as a dear friend as well, and this was certainly a time in her life when she needed friends.

Randee's parents had been dead nearly six years now, and it felt good to be watched over and worried about by someone again, just a little bit. Randee often thought that Lani probably had enough love in her to mother every lost soul on the island. Her natural intuition, no-nonsense advice, and extra-large heart had been incredible blessings to both Randee and Rorey. Since she had come into their lives, the world didn't seem quite so lonely anymore.

Randee found the fresh pot of coffee that Lani had left for her in the kitchen. Grateful for a few minutes of quiet while Rorey was asleep, she poured herself a cup and sat down at the kitchen table. She needed time to sort out what had happened in her meeting with Cord Barrett.

One impression dominated her memory of the man: strength. That was odd, considering he was recovering from a major accident. Yet somehow, instead of making him appear vulnerable, the cast on his leg and the crutches served to highlight that strength, as if to prove that he wouldn't be defeated by the burdens that dragged down other men.

The image of him standing before her as he had that morning suddenly intruded into her mind; his body nearly naked, a slight sheen of sweat glistening on his taut torso, turning his body into a piece of living sculpture. Her heart beat faster at the memory of being so close to him, close enough to reach out and touch his hot bare skin. For just a moment, she allowed herself to imagine how that heat might have felt under the tips of her fingers, how the solid planes of his torso would have resisted the pressure of her hands—

Randee pushed the vivid fantasy from her mind. She was not used to being affected by any man's physical presence in such a disturbing way, and she didn't like the strange, out-of-control feeling that being with him had inflicted on her. She certainly wasn't going to make it worse by imagining things.

Yes, it was true, Cord Barrett was everything he was rumored to be: stubborn, irritating, bullheaded, contrary—and very attractive. And whether he liked it or not, she and the defiant Mr. Barrett were partners now. It wouldn't be easy, probably not for either one of them. But she would make it work. She really had no choice. Cord didn't know it, but she was in as much of a bind as he was.

Randee sipped the fragrant coffee. Rich Kona coffee, grown locally on the Big Island but still expensive, was one of the luxuries she permitted herself. There weren't too many of them these days. She was very careful about money. She had to be, now.

A few years ago, when she'd been married to a man the newspapers had called "the most important force in the Honolulu business community this decade," being cautious with money hadn't been necessary. In fact, J. Maxwell Turner had encouraged her to spend money on herself. For Randee, overcoming her natural tendency toward thrift and practicality hadn't been easy. But Max had insisted that, as his wife, she had an important role to play, and she must look the part. Since she loved him, and wanted to please him, Randee tried to live up to his expectations.

He insisted that her clothes be the latest fashions and come only from the most exclusive shops in Honolulu, Los Angeles, or New York. Whenever he returned from one of his frequent business trips, he brought her a piece of jewelry: a ring, a necklace, or a bracelet. Many times the pieces were too extravagant and showy for Randee's conservative taste, but they were always expensive. That she knew for certain, because Max always made a point of mentioning their cost, as if that alone should make them beautiful.

After a year's worth of gifts, Randee had begged him to stop. She told him she already had more than she would ever be able to wear, that she didn't need such expensive presents. She smiled ruefully at that memory. Of course, she hadn't known then that those expensive, glittering baubles would turn out to be the key to her survival.

Randee poured out the last of her coffee, which now somehow tasted cold and bitter. She rinsed out the cup and put it by the sink, then investigated the small refrigerator for something quick for lunch. She found some tuna salad that Lani had left for her and began to pick at it without enthusiasm.

There was no time now to dredge up the past. Not that there was ever any way to really escape it, either. The memories of the last two and a half years were a part of her every day, and she couldn't change that. But for Rorey's sake, she could not dwell on those memories. She had to move on.

Her focus now had to be on only one thing: the *Kona Breeze*. That was the only thing J. Maxwell Turner had left behind him, besides painful memories. Ironically, the only salvageable part of his so-called investment empire was a business he'd owned for only a few months and had never even seen, let alone run.

When that business became her own, so did its problems. When Randee examined the company's books, she discovered that although the business was profitable, producing a fairly healthy cash flow each month, there was a large balloon payment to the bank coming due in less than six months. After a long, anxious evening pounding her calculator, it was painfully clear to Randee that the operation would not produce enough money to pay the debt when it came due, and without her husband's clout she knew she would never be able to qualify for a new loan.

She began investigating new ways of increasing the *Kona Breeze*'s business. She had already examined and discarded a dozen unsuitable plans when she learned of Cord Barrett's dilemma, and that was when her idea was born. She had just enough money from selling her jewelry to provide Big Island Wings with the extra capital it needed to resume operation, but that would be her last chance.

Only when she had the substantial contracts from the major tour operators in hand would the *Kona Breeze* be a bankable enterprise, and only then would she be able to refinance the debt. With a low enough rate and long enough term, Randee knew she would be able to pay off the debt out of her monthly profits from the business, but unless she could convince the bank of that, all would be lost. Since the bank had a lien on all of the company's assets, if it decided not to give her a new loan, it could simply force her to sell everything to pay off the debt. If that happened, she and Rorey would be left with nothing at all.

At the time she'd conceived it, she'd considered her plan pure inspiration. But now, as her mind turned back to the man she'd met this morning, she wasn't nearly as sure that she'd be able to pull it off.

Perhaps she had made a terrible mistake. He didn't seem like the kind of man who could work with anyone, let alone a woman. Especially a woman for whom he had already managed to express his disdain. What was it he had said to her? The words came back to her as she'd heard them this morning, dripping with sarcasm— "I'll bet you always get what you want. Whatever money can buy."

Randee shook her head at the irony of Cord Barrett's bitter observation. *I had plenty of money when I was with Max. I had everything that money could buy. But never once did I get what I wanted.*

Four

"How the hell did I get into this mess, Scuba?" Cord paced the length of the lanai for what might have been the hundredth time that day, his crutches thumping with a hollow sound against the rough wooden decking. He came to the end and turned back again. "Just answer me that, will you? How?"

Scuba didn't answer. She had given up following her master's anxious path back and forth much earlier and now was content simply to watch him pace from a warm pool of sunlight in the far corner of the lanai. She yawned and put her head down on her paws.

The weather was the best it had been in a week. The hot, humid air that had made the last week insufferable was gone, and this morning had dawned with a cool, fresh feeling that made every breath a pleasure.

But Cord didn't notice the coolness in the breeze, the fragrance of the blooming flowers, or the promise of the bright blue sky. His mind was consumed with the decision he had made the day before. Was he really that desperate? Hadn't there been another choice?

But he already knew the answer to that question, just as surely as Randee Turner had known it when she came to call on him the day before. She'd hit the nail right on the head, without flinching. *You won't be able to stay afloat much longer.* He could still see the way her flashing green eyes had examined him, probed him, as if looking for some weakness within him, a weakness she could exploit for her own purposes.

He wished that was all he could remember about her. But that wasn't the way it was. Not by a long shot. Through the long hours

of last night, as he struggled to find a comfortable position between sheets drenched with the sweat of the breathless tropical
night, images of Randee Turner had tortured him in other, far
more primal ways.

Her long, tan legs that looked smooth to the touch. The swell
of her full breasts with each breath. The classy tilt of her head
as she presented him with her blasted offer, in a voice that was
like a long, cool drink on a warm, sun-drenched beach.

Even as the words she spoke had infuriated him, her voice had
aroused within him other passionate responses, responses of a
very different nature: a low, dark aching that started deep in his
belly and spread relentlessly down through his loins; a smoldering
heat of need; a heavy pooling of desire that had found no release.

These were the things that had tormented him through the
night, long after his mind had wearied of the subject of his un-
wanted partnership with this woman. His body's responses had
remained undimmed by his mind's agony.

But now, as he paced his creaky lanai in the bright sunlight of
the late morning waiting for Randee Turner, Cord's focus had
turned from the heated thoughts of the long night to what the
woman would be bringing with her. Their new partnership agreement. Like it or not, he was going to be seeing a lot of Randee
Turner.

She was intelligent, no question about that, that much had been
obvious. And ambitious. Yes, very ambitious, and very interested
in what he could do to help her attain those ambitions. Just like
another woman, who had used him for all he was worth, then
stabbed him in the back with a smile on her exquisite face.

Randee Turner came from the same mold. He knew her type
very well, far better than she realized. He had her number, no
question about it. What frosted him was that it didn't make a
damn bit of difference after all, because he needed her. It was as
simple as that. The sooner he could make himself accept that
bitter truth, the better off he would be.

Scuba snuffled softly in her sleep, and Cord leaned against the
railing to give his sore leg a much-needed rest as he settled down
to wait for his new partner.

* * *

Randee slowed the van down to a crawl as she negotiated the rutted road. She knew that as soon as she rounded the next corner, she would see the clearing where Cord Barrett's house stood. She glanced for the tenth time at the van's clock. 11:40. She was twenty minutes early, and to be too early was probably as bad as arriving late, but there was no way to turn the van around on this narrow road. *Well, the sooner we get this over with, the better,* Randee told herself, but she sure wasn't convinced.

Even at her slow speed, the house came into view sooner than she would have liked. Randee hadn't eaten breakfast this morning, and now her stomach was churning, but she knew it wasn't from hunger. It was fear.

Yesterday, she'd gotten Cord to agree to their partnership, but what would happen today? What sort of mood would she find him in this morning? Would he be any more reconciled to his situation? Probably not. From what she'd seen of the man yesterday, he didn't seem like the type who was given to changing his mind.

Randee reached the clearing and stopped the van. Cord was watching her from the lanai. She slowly turned the van around to face back toward town before pulling the parking brake and shutting the engine off. *What are you doing,* she asked herself, *planning your getaway?* She grabbed her briefcase from the passenger seat and unlocked her door. *Okay, pull yourself together. You know what you have to do. Let's close this deal.* She opened the door wide and swung her legs out.

The shapely pair of legs Cord remembered only too vividly from yesterday morning dropped suddenly into view. Cord swallowed, hard. As Randee Turner dismounted from the van's driver seat, her raw silk skirt pulled up high across her thighs, giving him a tantalizing glimpse of what he'd only imagined yesterday. Then her feet touched the ground, and she instantly smoothed the errant fabric back down into place. She looked up and her eyes met his, and Cord guessed that she had probably caught him staring.

Well, what of it? With legs like that, she was no doubt used to the attention. Probably expected it by now, would be insulted if he didn't notice. But Cord's attention was quickly diverted from the woman's legs to the briefcase she carried in one hand.

In that briefcase, he knew, were the documents that would steal his independence from him, the contracts that would change the way of life he had sacrificed everything to obtain. The life that he had built from practically nothing, and now he was going to hand over more than half of it to a stranger. Why? Simply because she could come up with the few miserable dollars that he could not, and so desperately needed.

She approached the steps leading to the lanai, but didn't mount them, as if she were waiting for some signal from him before coming any closer. He gave her none.

"Good morning, Mr. Barrett." She shielded her eyes with her hand and looked up at him, smiling warmly, waiting for his response.

"You know, I've got to tell you, nobody ever calls me that."

"All right, then, good morning, Cord."

Cord stiffened. That voice again. Hearing his given name on her lips shot images through his mind, explicit images of a hundred intimate situations in which he would relish the sound of her whispering his name, shouting it in ecstasy. But not today, no. Irritated at his seeming inability to control his response to her, Cord pushed the thoughts away. That wasn't what today was about. He needed to pay attention to what Randee Turner was saying.

"I've got the partnership agreement right here." Randee patted the expensive-looking case. "I've read it, and it's straightforward enough, or at least as straightforward as any legal document can be, I suppose. Here it is, if you're ready to take a look at it." She unsnapped the case and withdrew a thick stack of papers, offering it to him. "I expect you'll want your attorney to look it over as well." Cord waved the documents away with a callused hand.

"There's no point in my looking at those papers. I already know what they say."

Randee felt her nervousness increasing. "Ah, so I suppose you prefer that everything go directly to your attorney. Well, then—"

"No."

Randee pulled back the agreement, instinctively reacting to the hostility in the man's voice. Had he changed his mind? She took a deep breath and tried again. "You really should review them, Cord. I don't want to have any misunderstandings between us.

The agreement's not complicated; basically, it outlines the terms we discussed yesterday morning, the nature of our partnership—"

He silenced her with a glance. She suddenly wondered if he thought she was patronizing him. She searched for words to apologize, to smooth his ruffled feathers, but he spoke before she found them.

"Look, it says you're more or less bailing me out of this jam, right?"

"Well, yes," Randee was choosing her words with extreme care. "It specifically delineates which of your obligations I'm taking on—"

"And it says you get fifty-one percent of Big Island Wings, right?"

The anger in his voice was chilling, but there was no point in trying to dance around the truth. She wouldn't even begin to try. One thing was absolutely certain, Randee would no longer tolerate lies in her life, not from others, and certainly not from herself. She'd already lived with enough lies to last her a lifetime.

"Yes." Randee steeled herself and met his defiant stare straight on. "Yes, Cord, it does."

"That's all that matters to me. All the rest is just a lot of legal garbage." He turned and walked the few steps to the end of the lanai, looking off into the distance as if searching for something.

"In a way, I suppose you're right, Cord." Randee climbed the three steps to the lanai. "It really doesn't matter what the documents say, what fancy words the lawyers use. You and I have already agreed to the terms, and I think you're a person of your word. I know that I am." She waited for some acknowledgment from Cord, but none was forthcoming. "The only thing that really matters now is that we are going to be partners, and I, for one, am excited about that. We can do great things together, I'm sure of that."

Randee studied the taut interplay of the muscles in his back through the thin fabric of his T-shirt, trying to read his mood, as she waited for his answer. A long silence passed between them. Finally, she took a pen from her case and opened the partnership agreement to the final page.

"So you know what I say, Cord?" She clicked the pen open.

"I say to hell with all the legal crap. Let's just sign this damn thing and get to work."

Cord slowly turned around and looked at Randee. In his eyes she thought she saw begrudging amusement, and maybe even a flicker of respect.

"Is that what you say?"

In answer, she nodded and signed the agreement, supporting the papers against the rough railing of the lanai. Then she offered the pen to him. His hard blue eyes locked on to her, and she felt the challenge in them, that and something more. She met the challenge and returned it to him. She realized she'd been holding her breath, and she made a conscious effort to breathe normally again.

Suddenly, Cord broke the gaze and reached for the pen, and the rough tips of his fingers brushed against hers as he took it from her. Randee pulled back. In that instant of slight skin-to-skin contact, she'd felt as if a shock of electricity had passed between their fingers.

Cord picked up the documents and flipped through them, glancing at each page for only a few seconds. When he reached the last page, he signed the line with his name typed beneath it. He handed the stack of papers back to her. He watched in silence as she filed them back in her briefcase.

"Is that it?"

"That's it."

"Okay, then, *partner.*" Randee felt the sarcasm that dripped from the word, but a touch of humor and warmth was there as well. "When do you suggest that we get *our* helicopter out of hock?"

"How about today?"

The drive to the repair yard passed in awkward silence. As Randee maneuvered the van down the highway from Honaunau toward Kailua-Kona, she managed to steal a few surreptitious glances toward her taciturn passenger. He had pushed the van's passenger seat as far back as it would go to accommodate his plaster-clad leg, which was stretched out in front of him defiantly. In spite of the cast, his lanky frame was sprawled in the seat with an attitude of studied indifference. His crutches were carelessly tossed between the two seats, as if he had decided that he no longer needed them.

His attention appeared to be focused on the passing scenery, but she couldn't be sure what he was looking at from behind his dark sunglasses. The warm air blowing through the open window fingered through his shaggy blond hair.

Randee tried several times to break the silence. Now that they were partners, she wasn't willing to walk on eggshells every time she was alone with Cord. But her small talk about the weather went nowhere; Cord barely acknowledged she was even speaking.

Mercifully, they soon arrived at the small industrial park near Keahole Airport where the helicopter was being repaired. Randee parked, then faced the awkward moment of deciding if she should offer to help Cord get out of the van. She made her choice, but before she could reach Cord's side, he hopped out and slammed the door. She could see the tension in his body, a tension that made every movement into a warning. *Don't touch me* seemed to be written all over him. She turned away, hoping that he hadn't noticed her intention to help.

Randee pushed open the door to the tiny office and held it open in silence for Cord to enter. An overworked air conditioner chugged away in the window. A skinny young woman with thick glasses jumped up from her desk behind the counter and exploded into a gap-toothed grin.

"Cord! Great to see you!" She brushed back a wisp of her frizzy brown hair. "How's the leg?"

"Better." Cord slipped off his sunglasses and smiled at her. "Better every day, Angie, thanks for asking." To Randee's surprise, Cord's voice was warm and friendly. She certainly wasn't used to him speaking to her that way.

"So what's the occasion?"

"I've come to collect my copter, Angie."

"Uh, Cord . . ." Randee could see that the woman was getting flustered. "You know if it were up to me there wouldn't be a problem, but Bob says we've got to have—"

"Tell Bob he's got nothing to worry about. I've got the money this time." Cord started toward the door, then turned back.

For the first time since they'd left the van, Cord turned toward

Randee. "This is Randee Turner. She'll take care of the paperwork. I think I'll go have a look at the bird." Cord went out the door leading to the fenced yard behind the office. The door slammed behind him. Angie shook her head slowly and let go with a long, low whistle.

"Ooh, that boy can charm you and harm you in the same breath. And not hard to look at either, not at all." Angie shook her head again and reluctantly turned back to Randee. She seated her glasses more securely on her nose. "But of course, I'm not telling you anything. I would guess you certainly know all about that, right?" She examined Randee through her thick lenses, making no attempt to hide her curiosity. When Randee made no comment, she continued. "So, you must be Cord's . . . his . . . um . . ."

"Business partner."

"Partner? You've got to be kidding."

"Not at all. We finalized the deal this morning."

Angie's pale eyes widened in disbelief. "Please don't take offense, but Cord Barrett is the original loner. I just can't imagine him getting hooked up with any partner, especially not a—a—"

"A woman?"

Angie merely nodded and shrugged her bony shoulders in reply, an eloquent gesture that somehow managed to convey both her affection for and frustration with Cord Barrett.

"I know, Angie. Believe me, I know. I'm still getting used to the idea myself." Randee took her checkbook out of her briefcase. "So how much do we owe you?"

Cord slowly circled the helicopter, the rubber tips of his crutches soundless on the hot asphalt. Once, twice, three times he circled it. Everything looked perfect, freshly painted and completely restored, as though the accident had never happened. Too bad he couldn't say the same about himself.

He opened the door and stood for a moment, just staring into the cockpit. There was the instrument panel, so familiar to him that he knew he could find every switch and gauge on it blindfolded. Cord leaned his crutches against the side of the helicopter and heaved himself in, crawling over the copilot's seat to the pilot's side, carefully maneuvering his bad leg around the foot controls.

Cord settled into the seat, which molded itself to his body with an intimate fit born from countless hours of flight. His breath was coming heavy from the effort of getting into the cockpit, but he chose to ignore that. He leaned his head back and closed his eyes. For a moment, if only in his mind, he was free again.

Randee opened the office door, and a blast of warm air greeted her. She could see the helicopter out on the asphalt pad, which shimmered in the heat. A pair of crutches were leaning against the copter's side, but Cord was nowhere in sight. Randee began to walk toward the helicopter, and as she got closer, the glare off the copter's Plexiglas bubble shifted, and she could see that Cord was in the cockpit.

Randee approached the open door of the helicopter slowly. She could see Cord clearly now. Was he asleep? His hand rested back against the seat, his eyes concealed behind dark glasses. As she drew closer, she could see the steady rise and fall of his broad chest under the thin cotton of his T-shirt. Randee suddenly felt as though she were intruding on a private moment, one she had no right to be observing. She stopped and waited for him to notice her, but he didn't stir.

Randee's eyes traced the long line of Cord's body from the hollow of his throat down his muscled chest to his flat abdomen and lean hips. The fabric of his well-worn cotton shorts fit snug and easy over his thighs, one thick with muscle, the other encased in hard plaster. Without thinking, Randee moistened her dry lips with her tongue.

Suddenly, Cord lifted his head and looked at her, as if he had felt her eyes on him. Randee felt herself flush with color, but she kept her voice steady.

"So this is your copter?" She climbed into the copilot's seat.

"Yeah, here she is." He gestured dramatically toward the banks of round black and white dials. "The old girl and I have been through a lot together." When she didn't answer, Cord shot her an appraising glance, and his dark blond eyebrows arched over the dark circles of his lenses. "I take it you are not impressed?"

"No, it's not that," she answered honestly. "I guess I just don't know enough about helicopters or flying to even know whether

I should be impressed or not. But I'd really like to learn." *Just as long as we stay on the ground,* she added to herself.

"Well, since you are now the proud owner of fifty-one percent of this aircraft, please permit me to enlighten you. You are sitting in a Bell JetRanger 206B, which accommodates four passengers." Cord jerked his thumb at the four empty seats behind them. "You will note that on Big Island Wings, unlike some of our competitors, every passenger gets a window seat. A very important distinction, would you agree?"

"Yes indeed. Very nice." Randee suddenly realized that this was the first time Cord had ever smiled at her. The sight gave her a strange fluttering sensation deep in her stomach. For the first time since the two of them had met she sensed that Cord was starting to relax. He even seemed to be enjoying himself a little.

"Now this thing here is called the cyclic." Cord grabbed the handgrip of the control that curved up from the cockpit floor. "It controls the angle of the rotor system, while the pitch of the rotor blades is controlled by the collective, which is over here on the left—"

"Cord, wait a minute, hold it, please." She put up a hand to stop him. "I don't really want to know all this technical stuff. Tell me what our passengers will want to know—why should they spend their hard-earned money on flying with Big Island Wings?"

"Why?" Cord pushed his sunglasses up onto the top of his head and looked at her intently. "Why?" Randee thought she had never seen eyes quite that blue before, bright, iridescent circles surrounding mysterious, dark centers. "I'll tell you why."

Cord leaned back in his seat and looked out through the Plexiglas bubble that enclosed them. "Because there's nothing else like it." His eyes grew dark with memory and seemed to be focused somewhere far beyond the tarmac and the chain link fence that surrounded them here.

"When you're up there, you don't just see what you see on the ground. You see the islands as they used to be, before the hotels and the restaurants and the condos and the cars." He paused, and Randee suddenly became conscious of the sound of Cord's breathing, and her own. She waited, hoping he would continue.

"You see where lava poured from the earth and created new land. You see jungles so dense they've never been crossed by man.

You see pools and waterfalls so perfect and pristine they make your heart ache." Cord's voice dropped low, as if he were speaking only to himself. "You see what paradise must have looked like."

"Before the apple, I take it?" As soon as she'd said it, Randee regretted her feeble attempt at wit, afraid he might think she was laughing at him.

Cord looked at her with a strangely piercing gaze that seemed to pass right through her. "Yes, you're right. Before the apple." He fell silent.

Randee was astonished at the change in the man sitting beside her. He was probably the most roughhewn man she'd ever met, irritable, intractable—what had Angie called him?—the original loner. Yes, that name suited him. And yet at this moment she could feel a deep core of strong emotion running through him, something like tenderness, or possibly even reverence, underscoring his every word. What kind of man was Cord Barrett?

"You must really miss flying." For some reason she didn't completely understand, Randee wanted him to keep talking. The tiniest crack had opened in his granite facade, and she didn't want it to snap shut again.

"Yes." The single word spoke endless emotion.

Randee hesitated, debating whether to ask him the question that was uppermost in her mind right now. She decided to go ahead and ask.

"Would you tell me what happened? I mean, about the accident." There was a moment of silence, as if maybe he hadn't heard the question.

"There's nothing to tell." With those few words, Randee felt a heavy curtain drop between them. She instantly regretted her boldness. Cord pushed his sunglasses back down into place, the expression in his eyes now hidden by the dark lenses.

"Cord, I'm sorry, I didn't mean to—"

"Look, it's the oldest story in the book. I made a mistake, and now I'm paying for it. That's all there is to it." He twisted his body toward the aircraft door, as if he might climb out right over her. "Let's get out of here. I've got to give Bob instructions on getting this bird back to my tie-down at the airport."

Reluctantly, Randee climbed out of the helicopter. The brief moment of intimacy between them was shattered. She stood by feeling helpless as Cord eased his body out of the copter and reached for his crutches. Randee searched in her purse for her sunglasses, and by the time she found them, Cord had already reached the office door.

"Cord, wait—"

The door slammed closed behind him.

Five

Cord was determined to keep Randee at a distance. It was for the best, he knew that. She flipped his switch, no doubt about it, and that could be very dangerous. One thing he knew for certain; a man made bad decisions when he let his body do the thinking. He wouldn't make that mistake again. He'd learned that lesson the hard way.

But in spite of his best intentions, as they spent the afternoon settling his late accounts around town and preparing to get Big Island Wings in the air again, he felt his resolve beginning to slip. After taking care of the helicopter, Randee paid the rent on his space at the airport and his overdue insurance premium, and finally they stopped at the offices of the local newspaper, *West Hawaii Today,* to place the ad for the replacement pilot.

"Okay, what about this?" Randee blew a strand of dark hair away from her face and scrutinized her notes. Cord looked over her shoulder and wondered how anyone could read that strange chicken-scratching she called writing. She squinted at a word with curiosity, made a correction, then began to read out loud. "WANTED: Experienced Helicopter Pilot. Well-established tour operator will pay top dollar for right candidate. Please contact Randee Turner at . . ." Randee looked up at him quizzically. "What's the matter?"

"I think we should say 'Helicopter Pilot, Big Island experience required.' " Cord found himself looking at her mouth, especially her full lower lip. "I don't want some bozo who's never seen a volcano before in his life taking my copter down into Kilauea." His voice came out raspy. He wasn't really thinking about the new pilot. He was wondering how her mouth would taste.

"Fine. I don't have a problem with that. I'll make the change." Randee quickly erased, then scratched in the new words. She handed the clerk the paper. "Can we get this in tomorrow's paper?"

The clerk shook his head. "Day after."

Randee sighed and looked up at Cord. "Guess that will have to do."

"Guess so."

Cord watched her lean against the counter as she filled out the check to pay for the ad. Her hair was swept up on top of her head, exposing the delicate skin at the back of her neck. He imagined gently pulling her hair free, free to tumble down around her shoulders in a dark river of silk. Free to skim over hot, bare skin. The skin across his chest tingled with the imagined sensation.

"I'll wait for you outside." He turned and left the office without offering an explanation. He needed to get away, and quickly. In the parking lot, he sought shade from the tropical sun under the building's awning, but he knew that it wasn't the sun that was raising his temperature. Cord cursed the dark, heavy ache in his groin, an ache that was beyond his power to control.

He knew all about women like Randee Turner. Women who were accustomed to being in control. Women who used their beauty and their money to buy whatever and whomever they wanted, then discarded their acquisitions as soon as they tired of them. He knew about such women, and yet as much as he wished to be, he was not immune to Randee Turner.

But in spite of all that, he simply couldn't shake the feeling that there was something more to her, something different. She exuded a certain appealing determination, an inner core of steel hidden within her that was unexpected. In spite of the awkwardness of the afternoon, in spite of the resentment he'd felt as she bailed him out of his financial mess, he had to admit that he could feel himself starting to soften toward her.

In all honesty, he'd actually enjoyed being with Randee. Hell, this had been the longest stretch of time he'd spent with another human being for quite a while. He was probably just starved for human contact. All right, he could admit it. Maybe he was even a bit lonely. After all, for quite a long time his social interaction had been limited to small talk with his passengers before taking them up in the copter. And ever since the accident, he didn't even have that anymore. In fact, these days, all he had were one-sided conversations with Scuba, and Cord was beginning to suspect that even she was getting tired of him.

But today had been different. Randee just would not let him be. She ignored his silences and his rude answers, and asked his opinion on everything, then always told him her own without his asking to hear it. She seemed intent on involving him, talking to him. Hell, maybe she really took this partnership thing seriously!

Randee emerged from the newspaper office and scanned the parking lot for Cord. She spotted him leaning against the wall of the building near where the van was parked, crutches against the wall a few feet from him, as if they'd been left there by someone else. She walked quickly across the lot. She considered asking why he had left in such a hurry, but decided against it. Where Cord was concerned, she was learning to be careful with questions.

"Well, that's done." She waited for a reply, but none came. "That's about all I had on the agenda for today. Is there anything I've missed?"

"No, I think that's about it. And now that you've seen everything to do with Big Island Wings," Cord said as he reached for his crutches and tucked them under his arms, "I'd like to take a look at the other half of our business."

"What?" His answer took her by surprise. All day long she'd been certain that he wanted to get rid of her as soon as possible.

"Take me to the *Kona Breeze*." Cord opened the van's passenger door.

"Sounds good to me. I'd really like for you to see it." Randee hesitated for a moment with the keys in her hand. She checked her watch. "But would you mind terribly if I stopped by my house to check in first? It's not far, and I've been gone longer than I expected to be."

Cord studied her face, searching for meaning. "Sure. No problem." He got into the van. This was probably her way of warning him to keep his distance, of putting him in his place. Now he'd probably have the pleasure of meeting her rich husband. For no good reason, the thought of her belonging to another man, of another man touching her, made his gut ache.

He looked over at her piloting the van up into the hills above Kailua-Kona. Again he had the urge he'd felt earlier to see her with her hair down. His fingers twitched as he imagined the feel of that dark, thick mass wrapped around them, the cool silk entwined with his warm fingers.

Randee turned onto a narrow, twisting street, then right onto an even narrower street. About halfway down the block she pulled the car into the open carport of a small house. "Here we are."

Cord was confused. This wasn't at all what he'd expected. He had assumed they would end up in one of the gate-guarded communities high above Kailua-Kona, neighborhoods he'd seen only through the fences. He certainly did not expect to find Randee living on this lovely but quite modest street lined with plumeria trees in full bloom.

Randee must have read the surprise in his eyes. She flushed slightly and shrugged. "I know the house is a little run-down, but we like the view. The landlord has promised to replant later this year."

Landlord? Cord was even more confused. Randee and her wealthy husband were renting this little place? Things were not making sense.

She opened her door. "Would you like to come in and meet Rorey?"

"Sure." The last thing Cord wanted to do was meet her husband, but there was no polite way to decline, and besides, his curiosity about Randee's life was beginning to drive him crazy. He wanted to know more, even though he knew the details would only serve to frustrate him further. He busied himself with gathering his crutches and the awkward task of getting out of the car. Randee had the front door unlocked by the time he reached it.

"Rorey! Rorey darling, I'm home!" Randee dropped her purse on the kitchen table. "Where are you, sweetheart?"

Great. She was really laying it on now, making sure he got the message loud and clear. Cord steeled himself to be pleasant to a man he already knew he would detest. He drew himself up to his full height, suddenly very conscious of his crutches, wishing he could just pitch them away and walk in unassisted. He opened the screen door and stepped inside the house.

At that moment, a little blond-haired, blue-eyed toddler came running into the room and wrapped himself around Randee's leg. "Mama!"

Randee swept the little boy up into her arms and kissed him. "Hello, sweetheart, I missed you today!" She hugged him again, even more fiercely, then relaxed her hold. "Rorey, this is Cord. Cord, this is Rorey." The child regarded him with a curious, cautious stare.

"Hi, Rorey." Cord's mind was racing. So this was Rorey! But where was his father?

A stout Hawaiian woman hurried into the room. "Rorey's been asking for you all day, Randee. We expected you earlier." She turned toward Cord, dark eyes twinkling with mischief. "And who is this?"

"Auntie Lani, please meet my new partner, Cord Barrett. He's the one I told you about."

"Oo, Randee!" Auntie Lani clasped her hands together in front of her ample bosom. "But you never told me he was so handsome."

"Lani!" To her embarrassment, Randee felt her cheeks burn with sudden color.

"Yes," Auntie Lani looked Cord up and down with obvious approval. "Very good-lookin' man." She nodded for emphasis. "Nice to meet you, Cord."

To her surprise, Randee saw Cord's face turn as bright red as her own felt, but his reply sounded warm and sincere. "Very nice to meet you, Auntie Lani." He smiled charmingly at Lani, but when he glanced back at Randee, she could see that there were unasked questions in his eyes. She wondered which ones he would have the nerve to ask her.

Rorey wiggled to be put down, and Randee lowered him to the floor. She watched closely as the little boy ran to Cord's side and slowly put an experimental hand out toward the cast on his leg.

"Kind of funny-looking, isn't it?" Cord noticed his interest and moved his crutch aside to let Rorey get a better look at the cast. He bent down to talk to Rorey as best he could with the cast. "Feel's pretty weird, too. Go on, it's okay, you can touch it." Cord's voice was low and conspiratorial in tone, as if he were letting Rorey in on a big secret. Rorey smiled and rubbed the white plaster curiously, then looked up at Cord with his innocent blue gaze.

Randee let Rorey inspect Cord's cast for a minute before she spoke. "Well, we'd better get on our way, while it's still daylight." Randee opened the front door. "I'm taking Cord down to Keauhou Bay for a quick look at the *Kona Breeze,* but I should be back in time for dinner." Randee knelt down and kissed Rorey, who was still enthralled with this big man's funny leg. "I'll be back soon. Be good for Auntie Lani."

Auntie Lani swept Rorey up into her sturdy arms. "I'm making my specialty tonight, *laulau* chicken." She looked pointedly at Randee, and then at Cord. "There will be plenty, for sure."

Randee sighed silently. She got the point. There was no arguing with Lani when she got an idea in her head. "Would you like to come back for dinner, Cord? Lani's *laulau* chicken is wonderful." Of course, she knew he would decline. The last thing Cord Barrett wanted was to spend any more time with her than he absolutely had to. She hoped he would be civil about turning her down, for Lani's sake.

"I'd love to." Cord smiled broadly, as if he were sincerely pleased by the invitation.

"You would? Are you sure?" Randee heard the disbelief in her own voice and felt her face grow hot again. "I mean, that's great. Lani's one of the best cooks on the island, or so everyone tells me. I mean, I think she's great, too." *What's wrong with me?* Randee thought. *I'm acting like a nervous teenager.* Surely she could handle a simple dinner with her new partner.

"You won't be disappointed, Cord, I promise. One thing Lani knows for sure is cooking." Lani smiled and winked at Cord. "Sometime I tell you what the other thing is." She laughed and urged them out the door. "You two get going now, so I can finish up in the kitchen. Rorey, tell Cord bye-bye."

It was just before sunset, when Randee parked the van in her regular space in the parking lot at Keauhou Bay. The *Kona Breeze* drifted gently back and forth on the lines that anchored it to the rough wooden dock. She opened the door and paused for a moment, watching the big trimaran. As she always did, she felt a surge of pride in the boat, a sense of ownership that she hadn't felt since the early days of Paradise Fragrances. That was long before she'd let Max Turner steal it from her, just as he'd stolen everything else from her. The *Kona Breeze* belonged to her, and nothing was going to take it away.

Cord had maneuvered around on his crutches to the front of the van and was stopped short by the expression on Randee's face. The gentle breeze off the water was stirring the tendrils of hair that had escaped around her face, which was shining with a glow he hadn't seen there before. He followed her gaze to the handsome trimaran waiting at the dock. Randee's eyes betrayed an involvement, a caring, that made her even more beautiful than before.

Randee suddenly seemed to realize he was watching her, and she laughed nervously. "There she is. Let me give you the tour."

"After you." Cord followed behind, and he recklessly let himself enjoy the movement of her firm, rounded bottom leading him forward. To his surprise, when she reached the boat, she stepped out of her high heels and nimbly jumped aboard with her shoes in hand. From some hidden spot on board she produced a well-worn pair of boat shoes and slipped them on.

"Forgive my outfit, but I was dressed for business today, not boating." With a show of strength that surprised Cord, Randee pulled the boat up close to the dock, closing the gap between the boat and the dock. "Can you manage coming aboard with those crutches?"

"No problem." Cord planted the tips of his crutches on the deck and managed to swing aboard the boat without a slip. He looked around. "This is some boat."

"Yes, she certainly is. Fifty feet in length and nearly thirty feet across. Not the biggest boat on the island, but by far the best designed, if I do say so myself." Randee's pride was evident in every word she spoke. "The *Kona Breeze* was custom-built for her job, and she does it well." She gestured toward the rear of the boat, where a wide staircase provided access to the water. "She's designed to make getting in and out of the water easy for everyone. Of course, the kids prefer the waterslide."

"Waterslide? What waterslide?"

"If you can negotiate the steps to the upper deck, I can show you."

"I'm not completely incapacitated, my dear partner. Just slowed down a little."

Bypassing the steep crew's ladder, they climbed the passenger stairway to the top. By the time they reached the open-air upper deck, the sun was sinking below the horizon. They walked back to where the deck gave a spectacular unrestricted view of the sunset. Silently, they watched the fiery ball sinking into the ocean.

Although Cord kept his eyes on the spectacular sunset, his mind was awash in questions he wanted to ask Randee. But one particular question stood out above the rest, a question to which he needed to know the answer right away. When he could no longer wait, he broke the silence.

"You've got yourself quite a good-looking little boy."

"Thank you. He's very special." Randee turned and smiled at him, a smile that was filled with a depth of love that made him ache. Then she turned back to the last rays of the sunset. Then, more quietly, "He's the most important thing in the world to me."

Cord waited before he continued, turning words over in his mind, wondering how best to ask the question. Unable to find a subtle way, finally he just said it straight out. "So where's his father these days?"

She met his eyes directly with an expression that asked for no pity. "His father's dead. I'm a widow."

For a moment, Cord was shocked into silence. Inwardly he cursed himself for his tactless blunder. "I'm so sorry, Randee, I didn't realize—"

She raised her hands and silenced his embarrassed outpouring.

"Cord, there's no reason to apologize. That's a perfectly reasonable question. Of course, you didn't know. There's no reason you would have."

"Still, I'm sorry."

Randee crossed her arms over her chest, trapping her hands tight underneath her arms. "Besides, the situation is a little more complicated than what you're probably thinking. You shouldn't waste a lot of sympathy on me. I'm not exactly a grieving widow."

"What do you mean?"

"Rorey's father and I were—well, we were in the process of divorce when he died."

"What happened to him?" Cord was puzzled. Although Randee's words were calm, he could sense an undercurrent of emotion that went beyond her matter-of-fact manner.

"Car accident. He was killed instantly."

"I see."

"Of course, it was a terrible thing, especially for Rorey, who is growing up without a father. But as for me and Max—we had not been happy in our marriage. Our life together was already over, had been for quite some time. Now I just have to concentrate on being the best mother I can be to Rorey."

Cord nodded, repeating her words over in his mind. She wasn't fooling him with her cool attitude, not for a minute. There was hurt there, real pain, pain that he could feel. Cord could feel the ache she was carrying inside her, and he knew beyond a doubt that there was much more to that ache than the simple story she was telling.

He wanted to know the rest of her story, but he wouldn't pry. He knew about privacy, maybe better than anyone. He wouldn't dream of violating hers. And yet, he was surprised at the pain he was feeling in response to her secret. It had been a very long time since he had let himself get involved in another person's private life. He couldn't afford to let himself start now. But damn it, he could feel himself being pulled into this woman's feelings.

Randee watched the very last sliver of sun disappear beneath the shimmering blue Pacific. She could feel the tension emanating from Cord, and she was determined to sweep it away. She had already told him more about herself than she should have, more than he needed to know. There was no need to muddy their already complicated partnership with a lot of messy personal history. And it was messy. And painful. Even the skeletal facts she had shared with him had hurt to repeat. She forced a smile and turned back to him.

"Well, I suppose Auntie Lani is probably wondering where—" The look in Cord's eye stopped her in mid-sentence. For an instant, she felt as if he were looking into her soul, looking right through the simple answers and pat explanations she had constructed around her heart like a high, solid wall. The feeling was like a sudden squeezing sensation in her chest that left her momentarily without breath.

Very slowly, he lifted one hand to her throat, and she could feel the rough pads of his fingertips against the soft skin just beneath her jaw, slowly stroking, leaving trails of flame along her throat with the firm friction of his touch. For an exquisitely long minute they stayed like that, no words spoken, unmoving except for the gentle motion of Cord's fingers, their gaze locked together.

Then his hand slowly left her throat and his arms encircled her in a sinewy circle of strength that drew her close to him. Randee felt the warmth of his hard body radiating from him like the tropical sun at midday.

She tried to speak again, to form words that would make sense, but before any sound escaped, Cord silenced her with his mouth. His kiss was slow and gentle, but in it she could feel the heat and need of his mouth. In only an instant, she knew that she wanted more. She needed more. Without conscious thought, her arms entwined around his solid shoulders, her fingers hungrily tracing the interplay of sinewy muscle beneath the fabric of his T-shirt.

Cord's response to her touch was instantaneous. The heavy heat that had pooled in his groin flamed hotter, his body tightening and swelling in response to her eager, searching fingers.

He had intended to kiss her, just kiss her once and be done with it. But the moment for that kind of restraint had long passed. Now he had to taste her, had to experience the sweetness he knew he would find within her mouth. He kissed all around her full mouth, then explored the outline of her lower lip with a sweep of his tongue. A low moan came from somewhere deep within her, a sound of desire, and her lips parted to receive him. Cord took her mouth fully with his own, exploring the secret warm places.

She eagerly crushed up against him, and the pressure of her soft, yielding body against his own made him painfully aware of the hard, pulsing strength that was trapped between them, a throbbing need that grew stronger and more demanding with each beat of his heart.

Suddenly, Cord knew with absolute assurance that he could not let this happen. He would *not* let it happen. No matter how strong his desire, or how willing this woman appeared to be, he would not let this situation get out of control. Randee was emotionally vulnerable, he could sense that, and he would not let that lead her into a decision she would regret, no matter how strong their desire.

He broke away from her mouth with a ragged groan. It took all the willpower he possessed to put his hands on her shoulders and gently move her back to put some distance between their aching bodies.

"I'm sorry, Randee." He wanted to say more, but the hurt and confusion in her eyes stopped his words in his throat. He longed to move his hands from her shoulders, to let his fingers trail slowly down the silk of her blouse to where her breasts rose and fell with each deep breath. He wanted to undo the buttons, to slip his hands beneath the fabric and touch and explore and feel her nipples tighten beneath his searching fingers. But instead, he took his hands away and let them hang awkwardly by his sides.

"I'm sorry," he said again, feeling the terrible inadequacy of the words. "Thanks for showing me the boat." He turned away and reached for his crutches, forcing himself to avoid her eyes. The last thing he needed was to get any more involved with Randee Turner than his desperate circumstances had already forced him to be, the rational part of his mind knew that for certain. He must not forget that.

Randee watched Cord position the crutches tightly underneath his arms and searched for words, but she found nothing to say. Her throat felt hot and dry.

"I'm afraid I'll have to take a rain check on dinner." His voice was cool and even; how could he be so controlled? Didn't he feel what had flamed up between them so suddenly?

"But—"

"I'm not thinking straight. This has been a long day for me, Randee. The most activity I've had since my accident." The corners of his mouth turned up in the slight echo of a smile. "My doctors would chew my butt out if they knew what I'd been up to today." He began to make his way toward the stairway to the lower deck.

"How—how will you get back home?"

"Don't worry about me. I'll find my own ride." He began the slow descent down the stairway. He paused, and looked back, meeting Randee's eyes but betraying little emotion. "Please apologize to Auntie Lani for me. I'll really miss trying her *laulau* chicken." He disappeared down the stairwell.

Randee stood rooted to the deck as still as if she were a part of the boat, a mast or stanchion. When she regained the ability to move, she ran to the edge of the deck and looked down to the dock. In spite of his crutches, Cord was already off the boat and halfway up the dock to the parking lot. As he rounded the corner and disappeared into the night, Randee gradually realized that regardless of the warm air of the balmy tropical night, she was trembling.

Randee's knees felt weak, and she sat down in the captain's chair that faced the boat's wheel. She searched her memory, trying to find a time, a place where she had experienced what she was feeling tonight.

But she already knew the answer. Tonight when Cord Barrett had held her in his arms and kissed her, her lips had burned for more, more of his mouth, more of his kisses. When she had felt the hard lines of his body against her own, she'd longed to be touched by him, touched in secret places, in intimate ways. Even now her skin carried the memory of where his fingers had touched her.

She'd never felt what she'd felt tonight. She'd never experienced desire blooming within her, like a tiny flame fanned into a roaring fire, a fire that threatened to consume her with its heat. No, she had never felt that with her husband, nor with her only other lover, the quiet dental student she'd lost her virginity to during her junior year of college.

But somehow tonight, a man she barely knew had brought something to life within her, something she had not even dreamed existed. And that realization scared her to death.

Six

For the sixth time that morning, Randee pulled back the lacy white curtain that covered her kitchen window and looked toward the street. Still no sign of Cord. She let the curtain drop. She checked the kitchen table again. Yellow pads, sharp pencils, a calculator, and a pitcher of ice water were all in place, making the table resemble an impromptu conference room. All business. Which was exactly what she wanted.

Three days had passed since that night on the boat, and she had not seen Cord even once. Their few phone conversations had been brief and businesslike, sticking strictly to the necessary details of getting Big Island Wings back in the air. To her relief, he didn't make any reference to what had happened between them the last time they were together, and she certainly wasn't going to bring it up.

Randee was grateful for the brief cooling-off period. She had used the time to analyze what had happened that night on the boat, and in her most logical manner, she had managed to convince herself that it was all some kind of aberration. Just a simple chemical reaction between two people and a romantic tropical sunset. Perfectly understandable under the circumstances, but absolutely the kind of thing that they were both better off pretending had never happened. It certainly must never happen again.

And she had done a good job of pretending that it had never happened, at least during the day. But the nights were a very different story. Just this morning, she had awakened quite early with a dream so vivid that its striking images still lingered in her mind.

In the dream, she and Cord were on a boat, not the *Kona Breeze* this time, but an outrigger canoe of the same ancient Hawaiian design that had been handed down from father to son through countless generations. She sat behind him in the canoe, watching the interplay of the rippling muscles in his bare back as he paddled through the surf. She did not paddle, but instead sat quietly waiting for them to reach their destination. It seemed completely natural that, like Cord, she was naked to the waist, with only a colorful *pareau* wrapped around her waist. Her breasts were warmed by the tropical sun and her hair was loose and skimmed her bare shoulders.

Next in the dream, she lounged on the warm sand of a deserted beach, watching as Cord pulled their canoe up onto the sand a few yards down from where she waited, waited for him to come to her. When the sleek, handsome vessel was secure, safe from the waves lapping on the shore, he turned and moved slowly toward her, powerful feet digging into the sand, never once taking his eyes from her.

Then he was standing above her, all tawny golden skin and taut muscle. She stretched luxuriously on the sand, waiting for him, knowing that he would soon come to her, that very soon she would know all of him. Then without speaking a word, he knelt down beside her and slowly put his mouth to her right breast, touching her only with his lips, teasing her nipple into a hard peak of pleasure—

The sound of the doorbell interrupted Randee's reverie. She stopped at the mirror in the hall before opening the door. To her embarrassment, her cheeks were flushed with the memory of the dream. She forced herself to take a couple of deep breaths. The doorbell rang again. She brushed her hair back out of her eyes and opened the door.

Cord had thought that he was prepared to see Randee face-to-face again, that he would have no problem putting aside what had happened the last time they were together. But now, as she stood before him framed in the doorway, he knew that he'd been wrong. Dead wrong.

She was dressed more casually this morning, and to him, even more appealingly, than he'd ever seen her before, in shorts and a button-down short-sleeve cotton blouse of bright teal. Her khaki shorts were cuffed a discreet few inches above the knee, and they were elegantly tailored rather than tight. The colorful shirt as well was comfortably sized, not clinging or revealing, yet somehow the overall effect was more devastatingly sexy than if she'd answered the door wearing the very briefest of string bikinis.

"Good morning. Looks like just another crummy day in paradise." *Brilliant, Barrett,* he chided himself. *Great opening repartee.*

"Good morning. You're late." In spite of her words, her voice carried no reproach. Instead, her voice had a husky quality that brought a surge of sensual images to Cord's mind. Her hair was down, and the effect was even more appealing than it had been in his imagination, a thick fall of silk with the rich color and shine of koa wood.

Her eyes held his, and for a moment they both just stood there, not speaking or moving, as if each were waiting for some sign, some clue from the other as to what would happen next. He was strangely conscious of his own breathing, and the taste of his own mouth, which now ached for her sweetness to fill it. To his relief, Randee finally broke the silence.

"Come on in. I've got everything set up in the kitchen."

She opened the door wider and stepped back to let him pass, but she did not move back quite far enough. Suddenly awkward on his crutches, he brushed against her as he entered, and the slight contact with her lightly perfumed body sent an immediate surge of heat to his loins. Cord gritted his teeth and tried desperately to ignore his body's response. He concentrated on getting himself settled at the table and his crutches stowed away. When he was safely seated, Cord looked over the precisely set table.

"Looks like you really know how to run a meeting."

Randee shrugged. "I ought to. I've run quite a few in my time. The applicants' resumes are in that folder in front of you."

Cord ran his fingertips over the crisp new manila folder but didn't open it. "Where were these meetings?"

"I had another business before, in Honolulu. Paradise Fragrances."

"Perfume?" Cord wrinkled his nose, and Randee could tell that even the thought of such a business was completely foreign to him.

"In the beginning, yes, that's how I got started. Selling all-natural perfumes by mail order out of my apartment while I was getting my MBA."

Randee went to the kitchen counter and poured herself a cup of coffee, although she didn't really want it, but at least it would give her something to hold in her hands. Even while gripping the cup, she noticed her hand was trembling slightly. Having Cord sitting at her kitchen table was suddenly making her very jittery. The sensual images from her early-morning dream kept intruding on reality, making it difficult to concentrate on the conversation.

Cord leaned back in his chair and folded both hands behind his head, watching her. "Mail order? I'm having a tough time trying to imagine you packing little boxes and sticking labels on them."

"The funny thing was that it was never supposed to be a real job. I just needed a way to help make ends meet until I graduated, and didn't want to wait tables. But my timing must have been right, I guess, because the business really took off. I had to hire a couple of my friends to help fill orders. By the time I was finished with school, I was able to open a retail store where we mixed custom fragrances for customers."

Randee sipped at the coffee, and the steam from the hot liquid wafted over her face, drawing little beads of moisture from her already-flushed forehead. The coffee had been on the burner since early morning, and she grimaced at its hot, bitter taste. "Eventually we carried a whole line of skin-care products. Natural cosmetics, too. In five years we had three stores, plus the catalog business."

"Sounds like a sweet deal for you. So why are you here if things were going so well? What happened to Paradise Fragrances?"

"I sold the business." Which wasn't really true, but it seemed like the best short answer she could give. The truth was much too complicated to get into. "I think we should get started on those resumes."

Cord opened the folder, and Randee poured the coffee down the sink and ran the water. She put both hands under the cool water for a moment, then touched her warm face with damp hands. Finally she dried her hands and face and turned back to the table, where Cord appeared to be engrossed in reviewing the resumes. He was flipping through them quickly, not spending more than a few seconds on each one.

She was behind him, and his head was bent forward as he thumbed through the stack of paper. His hair was slightly long in the back and curled against his collar. The breadth of his shoulders was emphasized by the soft, worn fabric of his T-shirt. Her fingers remembered the feel of those rock-hard shoulders.

The flushed feeling that had permeated her ever since awakening this morning had only intensified now that the man she'd dreamed about in such intimate detail was here with her in person. Silently, Randee counted to ten, then forced an all-business tone into her voice.

"Well, what do you think of our candidates?" Randee slid into the seat opposite Cord. "The two on the top with the paper clips are the ones that I felt would be the best choices. Experience, salary needs, everything seems in order." She felt a slight sense of relief at putting the stretch of smooth tabletop between them. "Besides that group, a few more came in today's mail."

Cord looked up, and his eyes were an icy blue. He picked up the sheaf of resumes in one big hand and dismissed them all with a single word: "Worthless."

"What?" Randee bristled with irritation, and she welcomed the feeling, vastly preferring it to the unsettled, confused way she'd been feeling since Cord had kissed her on the *Kona Breeze*. "And what exactly do you mean by 'worthless'?"

"Maybe 'dangerous' would be a better word. I'd be a fool to trust any of these copter jockeys with my aircraft, let alone some innocent tourists' lives."

"Cord, I'm not an idiot." She held on to her anger, glad to have a tangible, reasonable emotion to deal with. "I've spent some time on this process. The pilots I've selected all have excellent credentials—"

"For mainland flight, sure. Maybe even to fly fixed wing in the islands. But flying a helicopter on this island is different. This isn't like ferrying passengers from L.A. to San Diego." Cord smacked the table with one big hand, hard. The ice in the pitcher tinkled madly. "My God, Randee, this is the only spot on earth where you've got everything from desert to tropic to arctic conditions."

"What makes you so sure that you're the only one who can make this decision?" Randee stood up, now ready for a fight.

"This." Using both hands, Cord shoved his chair back from the table. He slapped the cast on his leg with a hollow thump. "This makes me sure. I've been up there, Randee. I've been flying these islands for fifteen years, and I still get surprised. This last surprise nearly killed me."

Cord slowly pulled himself upright without the benefit of his crutches, steadying himself with the edge of the table as he moved closer to her. His eyes were an unrelenting blue and granted her no mercy. "I know this island, and I know the weather. But I got tricked by a freak storm, and I made a mistake, a mistake that should have killed me."

When he spoke again, his voice was much softer, but each word was loaded with barely leashed emotion. "But I wasn't killed. I was lucky. The next guy, and his passengers, may not be as lucky. All I can do is make sure that whoever takes up my copter knows what the hell he's doing. I owe that to my passengers, and to myself."

Randee and Cord were now only a scant few inches from each other, and Randee could feel the emotion flowing from him like a palpable force vibrating from the whole length of his powerful body, waves of sensation crashing against her own frame. She felt a weakness in her knees and, for a moment, a breathless sensation that made her fear she might faint.

Without warning, Cord suddenly dragged her to him, strong arms pulling her tight against his hard chest. Randee opened her mouth in surprise, searching for words, but within seconds his hand at the back of her neck had brought her lips to meet his. He covered her protests with his own warm mouth. This time, no trace of hesitation or tenderness softened his actions, only a hot, searing need that demanded to be satisfied. His tongue plundered her mouth, shamelessly thrusting and exploring with strong, relentless strokes. Randee struggled against his strength for only a moment, then gave in to him totally, letting him take and take as he wished.

Her response to him was nearly instantaneous. Her arms wrapped around him with shameless greed, eager for the feel of his body under her fingers once again. Her breasts began to warm and swell, and suddenly she wanted, no, more than that, she *needed* the pressure of his hard chest against them. She rubbed against him, needing more than the feel of his body against hers separated by two thin layers of fabric. The slightly rough surface of his cast was warm as it rubbed against the bare skin of her leg, as if she could feel the heat of his flesh through the plaster.

He searched her mouth with a single-minded thoroughness that left her trembling, his peppery male taste exciting her more with each stroke. He broke away to plant hot, moist kisses all around her lips, which now felt tender and slightly swollen with pleasure. She endured it for only a few seconds before she pulled his mouth back onto hers again, and this time she was the one exploring him, their tongues now united in a dance of pleasure.

Cord's hand was at her right breast now, callused palm cupping the growing fullness through the layers of fabric. She squirmed against his work-roughened fingertips as they mercilessly teased her nipple, which was now tight and hard with pleasure. She heard herself moan into his open mouth. A tingling sensation radiated through her, a deep wave of heat that was spreading down from her breast to her belly and lower still to the most intimate center of her femininity.

Cord felt the nubby hardness of Randee's nipple under his fingers and heard the sound of pleasure that escaped from her throat. The heavy, throbbing pressure in his loins surged in response, and he answered her with his own groan of need and frustration.

He fumbled with the top button of her blouse, and to his surprise, she helped him unfasten it and the three below it, then pulled the blouse open. Cord sucked in his breath at the sight of her breasts, full and tempting in a simple lacy bra, the dark circles of her nipples visible through the sheer fabric. His fingers found the front clasp, and suddenly her breasts were freed to his hands.

Randee gasped as his fingers made first contact against her bare skin. The rough pads of his fingers trailed fire over the swell of her breasts, building to an exquisite white-hot heat as he reached her nipples, gently teasing and pulling them into hard points of pleasure. As his fingers worked their magic on her breasts, his tongue was in her mouth again, plundering and tasting her with abandon, spreading his peppery male taste to every secret hidden place.

Randee suddenly needed to touch him, to feel him underneath

her fingers just as he was now exploring her, driving her mad. She wanted to feel his hot, bare skin and begin to explore the mysteries of his body for herself. She slipped her hands beneath his T-shirt.

The skin of his torso felt just as she'd imagined it would, taut and smooth under her fingers. Her hands searched the planes of his chest until she found his own nipples, hard and flat and male. She teased them and they tightened in response. Her hands wandered down to the hard, flat ridge of his belly and the rough curls of hair that encircled his belly button.

Cord dipped his mouth low and tasted one breast. A searing bolt of pleasure shot through her, nearly bringing Randee to her knees. The sensations of last night's dream had been but a pale imitation compared to the exquisite torture of Cord's mouth on her nipple.

The fainting sensation she'd felt earlier returned, but this time instead of fighting it, she let herself yield to it, let herself sink totally into a new world of exquisite sensation.

A familiar sound entered the background of Randee's consciousness, but without registering any meaning or relevance. The sound continued, growing closer and louder, and eventually some distant part of her brain finally recognized it as the sound of her van pulling into the carport, but what did that have to do with anything when Cord's fingers and mouth were driving her crazy—

Outside, a car door slammed, followed by familiar voices, and suddenly, meaning dropped into place in Randee's mind. "Oh, no." She pushed Cord away from her breast and fumbled for her bra.

"What's wrong?" Cord looked confused but not the slightest bit alarmed.

"Quick, do something! Lani and Rorey are back from shopping!" Although she was moving as quickly as she could, Randee thought her voice sounded as if she were speaking underwater. She frantically buttoned up her blouse, first matching the holes to the wrong buttons, and then finally getting it right. She tucked the blouse back into her shorts, desperately trying to smooth herself into an appearance of respectability.

"Cord, what are we going to do?"

He gave her a slanting half-smile, but his eyes were dark with desire, a desire that made Randee's heart pound with her own hot need.

"Do? What are we going to do?" Cord gripped the edge of the table to steady himself as he moved back to his chair and sat down heavily. "Why, we're going to get back to work. What else?" He divided the stack of resumes, kept half for himself, and tossed the others on the table in front of the empty chair across the table. "You'd better sit down."

Seven

Randee sat down, knees weak and cheeks aflame. Her mind was trying desperately to understand what had just happened. How could she have let things between the two of them get carried away like that? She had never behaved like that before in her life! What was it about Cord that seemed to burn away all of her carefully constructed, logically conceived plans, leaving her at the mercy of powerful desires, desires she'd never even glimpsed before?

To her amazement, Cord was already flipping through the stacks of resumes, as if nothing had happened. But then he slowly raised his head and looked directly into her eyes, and the fire burning in his eyes told her that his desire was still there, still unsatisfied.

The front door opened, and Rorey ran in, followed by Auntie Lani carrying shopping bags. "Mama!" Rorey ran to Randee and climbed up into her lap. She hugged him tight, grateful for the reassuring and familiar scent of innocence that clung to him. Rorey allowed himself to be hugged for only a moment, before he wriggled free of her grasp to turn around and look at Cord. For a moment he stared across the table in thoughtful silence, then smiled and triumphantly pointed a chubby finger at him. "That Cord!"

"That's right, sweetheart. That's Cord." Randee stroked his smooth blond hair, willing her racing heart to slow down. "Lani, you remember my partner, Cord." Maybe she was the only one who could hear it, but Randee could tell that her voice was trembling a bit.

"Of course I remember. Too good-lookin' to forget." Lani gave

Cord a mischievous wink. "Lani don't forget a man like that."
Lani put her shopping bags down on the counter and unpacked
a few items. "So, have you two been workin' hard?" Her dark
eyes took in Randee's slightly disheveled appearance.

"Yes, ma'am, we have been. Real hard." Cord smiled that sexy
half-smile she'd seen a moment earlier and leaned back in his
chair. Lani smiled back knowingly.

Cord's gaze traveled from Lani to her, and Randee felt her face
grow a brighter shade of red. Lani was unpacking the rest of the
groceries with an elaborate nonchalance that didn't fool Randee
for a minute. Lani was a chronic matchmaker, and she'd made no
secret of her approval of Cord.

"Yes, Lani, we're trying to come to some kind of agreement
about this replacement pilot, but it hasn't been easy. Cord's being
rather—"

"Difficult?" Cord cocked an eyebrow at her. Randee tried to
meet his gaze without flinching, but when her eyes locked onto
his, she felt the pulse of desire that had faded with Lani's arrival
flare up within her again. She searched for words to answer him.

"That's one way of putting it."

Rorey wiggled out of Randee's lap and ran to Cord. Cord
picked him up on his lap with an easy gesture that suggested he
was completely at ease with children. He held the boy under his
arms and lifted him high in the air.

"Hey, buddy, you're cleared for takeoff." Cord gently moved
the boy from side to side and made a plane-engine noise. "You're
flying."

Flying!" Rorey squealed with delight, and Randee had to smile
at Rorey's enjoyment. Cord Barrett was a puzzle; how could someone so irritatingly contrary be so tender? And why couldn't she
get the thought of him out of her mind?

"Okay, little pilot, enough flying for now." Lani lifted Rorey
from Cord's arms and positioned him securely on one hip. "We
better go play at Auntie Lani's house and let your mamma and
Cord get back to their work."

Was there an odd emphasis on the last word? Randee couldn't
be sure about that, but there was no mistaking the broad wink
that Lani directed at Cord on her way out the door. Well, despite
Lani's best matchmaking intentions, this was going no further.

She would simply have to set Cord straight. The two of them had a business relationship, no more. She would just have to—

"You can relax now." Cord had retrieved his crutches from beneath the table and left his seat. He was behind her now, and his strong fingers were at the base of her neck, working the tension from the knotted flesh. "Come on, relax." The pads of his thumbs pressed powerfully against the cords of her neck. "I know you're shook up, but it's not like we got caught in a steamed-up car by your mother."

"No. No, it's not." Randee let Cord keep working on her tight neck and shoulders. She knew that she shouldn't, but it felt so good to have his massive hands on her, touching her, warming her. She suddenly realized that she wanted those hands everywhere.

"We're two adults." His voice was soothing, almost hypnotic, a slow-moving river of warmth that she longed to let herself drift away on. She felt herself begin to bend toward it, ever so slowly— but instead, Randee forced her mind back to cold reality. This was madness. She must put a stop to it immediately.

"Cord, stop. Please." She turned around to face him. He dropped his hands and gripped the handles of his crutches. "You're right, we are two adults. But more important than that, we're also business partners, and that's all we are. All that we can be."

When Cord didn't reply, Randee studied his face for clues, but his eyes had become guarded. She couldn't put a name to the emotion she saw there. "I'll admit I don't understand what's going on between us, but whatever it is has got to stop. I've got a business to run here, and I'm not going to lose control over some— some—"

"Uneducated, burned-out, bankrupt copter jockey?" Cord's voice was calm, but his eyes were dark and icy.

"That's not what I said, Cord." Things were happening so quickly, she wished she could get away by herself for just a few minutes, just long enough to understand what was going on. "Please, don't put words in my mouth. I'm not trying to hurt you. All I am trying to say is—"

"It doesn't matter what you say, Mrs. Turner. I know exactly what's going on. It's really very simple." Crutches thumping, Cord quickly crossed to the sliding glass doors that opened onto the lanai and a spectacular view of the Kona coastline. "Your body's telling you one thing and your mind's telling you another."

"Cord, that's not it at all, I just—"

"Don't bother playing coy with me. I'm in the same damn position as you are. I know exactly what you're feeling right now." He turned back to face her, swinging a step closer to her before he spoke again, dropping his voice as if they might be overheard. "I want you as much as I've ever wanted a woman. But do you think I'm going to risk everything I have just to hop in the sack with you?"

Randee gasped, but he spoke again before she could find the words to answer him.

"The answer is no. As I'm sure it is for you, too. There's too much at stake for both of us." Cord returned to his chair at the table and settled into it heavily, once again stowing the crutches beneath the table. "So since we agree on that, let's get back to work. I'd like to see the other group of resumes you mentioned. Maybe we'll get lucky."

"Maybe." Randee fought back a rising tide of anger as she went to fetch her briefcase.

They didn't get lucky that day, or the next, or the next. Each morning they convened over Randee's kitchen table to review what had arrived in their post office box the previous day. Although they received more than one hundred applications, virtually all of them well qualified in Randee's opinion, Cord found fault with each one. Randee was exasperated, but she knew that the tension between them went far deeper than their disagreement over the new pilot. By the third day, Randee had reached the end of her rope.

"Nope." Cord tossed the last page into the trash can by his chair.

"Cord, you barely looked at that one!"

"I saw all that I needed to see."

"Cord, it's time to make a decision." Her heart was beating faster, but she knew she had to put her foot down. "This whole process has become a waste of time. We've got to hire someone, and I mean now. We're losing money every day."

"We'll be losing a lot more than money if we hire someone who isn't qualified."

"Cord, I didn't want to have to say this, but ultimately, this is my decision. I own fifty-one percent of Big Island Wings, and we need a pilot." She picked up the small stack of pages she had put aside. "As far as I'm concerned, any one of these applicants will do just fine. I'll leave it up to you to choose which one, but I must insist that we hire somebody, today." Randee steeled herself for the burst of anger that she expected, but it didn't come. Instead, Cord's face had taken on an intensely thoughtful expression.

"Cord—"

"Don't say anything for a second." Cord closed his eyes tight for a second, then opened them and pounded triumphantly on the table. "That's it!" He threw back his head and let out a whoop that brought Lani and Rorey running into the room. "I knew there was an answer!"

"What? Cord, what is it? What are you talking about?" His response seemed so out of character that Randee briefly wondered if he'd lost his mind.

"Jason! Jason Clay! I don't know why I didn't think of it right off!"

"Who's Jason Clay?"

"Only the best damn helicopter pilot I've ever known. Outside of me, of course."

"Of course. But I'm afraid your qualifications are rather immaterial at this point." Randee struggled to keep the irritation out of her voice. "So what's the fabulous Jason Clay got to do with us?"

"Jason and I flew together years ago, when I first came to Hawaii. That's when I got to know him. He eventually went back home to the mainland, going after some girl, I think it was, and we lost track of each other for a few years. But things didn't work out between Jason and the girl, so he came back to the islands about five years ago. He's been flying for an outfit over on Kauai for the last three years. He's our man, no question about it."

"He sounds perfect, but why do you think Jason would want

to leave that job, drop everything, and move over here to the Big Island?"

"You don't have to worry about that." Cord's expression was irritatingly smug.

"What do you mean? Why not?"

"Let's just say that I did a favor for Jason once. He'll come. Trust me."

Jason was all that Cord had promised, and more. Because of Cord's obvious admiration for Jason, Randee had half expected, perhaps even feared, a replica of Cord's rather stubborn personality. But to her immense relief, the tall, dark-haired man with the square jaw and deep voice was as quiet and easygoing as Cord was bullheaded. From their first meeting at the airport, Randee was confident that she and Jason would get along just fine.

"Mrs. Turner?" The big man shifted his leather shoulder bag to his left side and extended his hand. "I'm Jason Clay. It's a real pleasure to meet you."

"Please, call me Randee." Randee's hand disappeared inside Jason's mammoth one, but she felt no threat from the disparity in their sizes. This man exuded calm.

"All right, no buttering up the boss, okay, big guy?" Cord's voice was gruff, but he clapped Jason around the shoulder with a warmth that surprised Randee. "This lady's not used to your fancy Texas manners."

"Actually, Jason, as you can probably tell, I'm not used to any kind of manners at all."

Jason's lips curved in a gentle and long-suffering smile that seemed to convey a wealth of unspoken history. "Well, Randee, knowing my pal Cord here as well as I do, that doesn't much surprise me. I'm afraid he's not much for the social graces."

Besides Jason's even temperament, there was another unexpected bonus: not only was Jason an experienced pilot, but he was an expert helicopter mechanic as well, and he insisted on performing all the maintenance personally on any aircraft that he flew. Randee had to admit it, Cord's choice had been a wise one. Within just a few days, Big Island Wings would be back in the air again.

* * *

"Here's the manifest for tomorrow's flights." Cord dropped the typed pages on Randee's table, which was still cluttered from their days of meetings. Late afternoon sunlight slanted across the shiny tabletop. Randee picked up the manifest and paged through it. Cord wasn't saying much, but she could tell he was pleased with something.

"Three full flights on our first day back in business." Randee smiled at him. "That's great. I guess you really do know what you're doing."

"I sure do. But I never thought I'd ever live long enough to hear you admit it." His voice carried just a hint of smug satisfaction, a husky tone that, for no rational reason at all, made her shiver with the memory of his hands on her bare skin. Randee pushed the memory away and tried to make her voice all business.

"Well, I'm sorry if I ever gave you the impression that I question your judgment. As far as Big Island Wings goes, you're the expert."

"Can we make that official?"

"What do you mean?" Randee tried to read his expression, but he wasn't giving anything away. Cord sank heavily into a chair and dropped his crutches beside him. He sat in silence for a moment, apparently studying the floor. Finally he looked up and met her eyes.

"Randee, I think that we need to put a little distance between us."

"I couldn't agree more." She felt herself stiffen. This was the first time that either one of them had mentioned, even obliquely, the intimacies that had passed between them. That certainly wasn't because the tension had gone away. In fact, quite the opposite had been true. Each day they spent together seemed only to heighten her uncomfortable awareness of him.

Cord shrugged, but the gesture was without apology. "I guess you've noticed that we seem to have a certain effect on each other . . ."

"I've noticed." Randee cut him off before he could elaborate. Noticed? She'd hardly been able to think of anything else. "And

I think a little distance, as you put it, is an excellent idea. Why don't you tell me exactly what you have in mind?"

Cord looked her over slowly before he spoke. Randee felt the heat of his gaze passing up and down her body, as if he really was considering telling her *exactly* what he had in mind. What they both had in mind. And it had nothing to do with business.

Finally, he spoke again. "I think we need a clear division of responsibilities. I'll take care of everything that has to do with the operations side of Big Island Wings. You stick to marketing the boat/helicopter packages and handling all the financial matters."

Randee nodded. "Okay."

Cord's full lips curved in a slight smile. "That way, we can each do what we do best, and I hope we can stay out of each other's, ah . . ."

"Hair." Randee jumped in before Cord could continue into more dangerous territory. With Cord, even innocent words could lead into hazardous situations.

"Right. We'll stay out of each other's hair."

Randee felt her cheeks burning. They both knew what Cord was talking about, and he was right. It was safer for them to avoid too much close contact. There was too much at stake here, for both of them. Neither one could afford to do anything that might jeopardize the ability to work together and, ultimately, the partnership itself.

But whatever the force was that was pulling them together, Randee could only hope that it would fade in time. It had to, because otherwise she was convinced it very well might destroy them both.

Eight

The next several weeks passed in a blur of activity, and Randee was grateful for the distraction that work provided for her. Although thoughts of Cord intruded frequently, she resolutely kept them at bay by reminding herself what was at stake right now: the *Kona Breeze*. In spite of her confusion, Randee knew for certain that she could not afford to be distracted from implementing her plan to save her business.

Randee devoted herself to wooing the large international tour operators, first on the phone, and then by spending a number of days in Honolulu making presentations to their managers and marketing directors. Her sales style was sincere and persuasive, and her pricing structure was aggressive. So far Randee had met with more success than she had dared hope for at this stage of her new venture.

As she walked back to her hotel after one particularly good meeting, she found herself remembering the period nearly eight years ago when Paradise Fragrances was just getting off the ground. She'd worked hard during those years, living in a tiny apartment on practically nothing, plowing all the profits back into the company to finance its growth. Even when the business began to prosper, expanding into three stores, she kept most of the money in the business.

Virtually her whole life had been her business. Looking back on it now, Randee realized that at the time she'd been remarkably innocent, even naive, to an extent that even her closest friends didn't realize. The image she presented to the business world was savvy and sophisticated; but when it came to the world of men and women, she might as well have still been back in high school.

That was why, she realized now, she'd been so easily deceived by the mature, reassuring manner of J. Maxwell Turner.

Randee crossed the large, airy lobby and punched the button to summon the elevator. The memory of Max had caused her positive mood from the meeting to evaporate, and she felt slightly sick to her stomach. She pushed the button again, angry at herself that even now, when he had been dead more than a year, Max still had such power over her.

As she waited for one of the elevators to complete its long descent from the high-rise tower, Randee scanned the hotel's directory of daily events posted in the glass case between the elevators. One of the items from the list immediately caught her attention: the Honolulu Children's Hospital Ball was being held this evening.

A soft chime announced the arrival of the elevator and she stepped on, awash in a sea of painful memory. She'd attended that fund-raising ball for a number of years when she'd lived in Honolulu. Randee had always had a soft spot in her heart for children, and she and her company had been big supporters of the Children's Hospital. In fact, Randee had always been proud of the fact that Paradise Fragrances contributed more to charity than many businesses ten times its size.

When she reached her room on the forty-third floor, Randee kicked off her shoes and settled into an overstuffed armchair near the window. She tried to enjoy the sunset and the arrival of purple dusk to the Waikiki skyline, but she could not stop the flood of unpleasant memories that was coursing through her tired mind.

In a way, it was charity that introduced her to J. Maxwell Turner. Paradise Fragrances was a sponsor of the annual Honolulu Children's Hospital Ball, and Randee always attended to show her support. That year, the old friend she'd recruited as her escort had come down with the flu, and so she was alone. She was making small talk with the strangers at her table when a man appeared at her side and asked her to dance. Tall, silver-haired, striking rather than handsome, he was smooth, charming, and attentive. After the first dance, he changed tables to sit by her for the rest of the evening.

The other people at the table all seemed to know him, and they treated him with the kind of deference that is usually reserved for the very famous or the very rich. In the course of the evening, Randee learned that he was *the* Max Turner of Turner Investments, one of the largest development and management companies in Hawaii. Turner Investments owned office buildings, hotels, restaurants, and other businesses throughout the islands; in fact, the company owned two of the three shopping centers where her own shops were located.

Yes, Max told her, he knew of Paradise Fragrances, and he knew of her as well. He'd seen the profile on her that had run in the business section of the paper last year. In fact, he'd been watching the growth of her company with interest. She was clearly a natural entrepreneur, he said, just as he himself was. But there was a time for business talk later. "Tonight," he said, "let's just dance."

That evening was the beginning of big changes in Randee's life. The next few months passed in a blur. Randee's experience with men had been limited to casual dates with her former college classmates, and nothing in her life had prepared her for a man of J. Maxwell Turner's sophistication. Nearly twenty years her senior, he courted her in grand style, showering her with gifts and attention that awed her. For the first time in her life she felt she was falling in love. When Max confided to her that he longed for children, her last concerns were swept away. She knew that they were meant to be together.

They were married only six months after their first meeting. The formal ceremony was attended by hundreds of J. Maxwell Turner's friends and business associates and the few close friends Randee had known since college. An old friend of her father's gave her away.

Randee was blissful. In preparation for the baby she hoped she would be conceiving very soon, she let the day-to-day management of Paradise Fragrances be taken over by her husband's company.

But only a few months after they returned from their European honeymoon, Randee felt things between them start to change. The rapt attention Max had focused on her during their courtship had evaporated overnight. In fact, her new husband didn't seem to have much time for her at all anymore. He began to travel for business more and more frequently and stayed away from home for longer periods. It seemed as if the only time they had together was when she accompanied him to his business associates' parties. Randee began to feel as if she were just another one of his possessions—one that he had already lost interest in.

Randee stood up and stretched. She was tired and hungry, which only enhanced the melancholy that had engulfed her since returning to the hotel. She was determined to shake herself out of her depression. She called room service for a bowl of soup and a sandwich, then took a quick shower. Afterward, even though it was early, she put on a light cotton nightgown and the white terry cloth robe she found in the closet. She needed to get some rest.

Room service arrived, and she ate quickly, hardly tasting the clam chowder and turkey sandwich. After dinner, she tried to distract herself with the newspaper, but after a few minutes she laid it aside.

Randee drew her knees up close to her body and tried to settle into a more comfortable position in the big overstuffed chair near the window. As she watched the never-ending activity of the busy Honolulu night that was unfolding far beneath her, she longed for the peaceful silence that night brought to the Big Island. She missed her son and the smell of his cheek when she came into his room to steal a last kiss as he slept.

But there was something else that she missed. Here, alone in the sterile comfort of her dimly lit hotel room, she could admit to herself what that was.

She missed being with Cord. In spite of her attempts to focus completely on work, in spite of her conviction that the success of this joint venture was the only way to ensure the survival of the *Kona Breeze,* in spite of knowing that the time she had spent with Cord Barrett had been confusing, exasperating, and disturbing—in spite of all those logical, sensible things, she found she still missed him.

It didn't make any sense at all. She knew that. But there was something about Cord, something that went deeper than just contrary nature and his bullheaded approach to problems. Something that went even deeper than the smoldering sexuality to which she'd felt her body surge in response.

There was a caring, protective side of him that she knew he

rarely revealed to others. She had seen it when he played with Rorey; and she had even sensed it, however guarded, toward her. And somehow Randee knew in her heart that this man, this ultimate loner, wanted desperately to care for someone else. Did she dare to let him care for her?

Randee looked at the clock and groaned. She had to try to get some sleep. Tomorrow morning was the most important presentation she had yet to make, to the hugely successful JTL Tours, a company that had pioneered the Hawaiian Islands as a vacation destination for Japanese tourists. If she won that contract, Randee knew she could boost her passenger level by as much as twenty-five percent.

She had done some calculating over breakfast this morning, and she knew she needed that contract if she was going to be able to convince the bank that her company qualified for a new loan. The balloon payment was coming due in only two and a half months, and without this contract, she would be hard-pressed to convince the bank of her creditworthiness, even with the other new contracts she'd already generated.

The answer was simple. She had to get the contract. There was no choice. The alternative was unthinkable.

Randee clicked off the light and climbed back into bed, weary, but certain she would never sleep. But the next sound that penetrated her conscious mind was the insistent beeping of her travel alarm, summoning her to prepare for her eight A.M. meeting.

"Kimo, we did it!" Randee jumped from her van and yelled her news as loudly as she could. She slammed the door and shouted again, this time toward the sky for all to hear. "We did it!"

Kimo, who had been the captain of the *Kona Breeze* for more than fifteen years, looked up from the line he was splicing to see his new boss running down the dock toward the boat, hair coming loose and flying in the breeze. Looking baffled, the big man put down the line and cupped a hand to his ear. "What? What are you talking about? What happened?"

Randee stepped on board, smiling widely. "We got the JTL contract! The first passengers arrive on Friday!" Spontaneously,

Randee hugged Kimo, but he didn't seem to share her excitement over the news.

"That's great, Randee." His voice was troubled.

She released him and studied his expression. "Kimo, is something wrong?"

Kimo cleared his throat and studied the deck beneath his feet for a moment. "There have been some problems while you were gone, Randee." His dark brown eyes met hers. "I didn't want to bother you while you were in Honolulu. I knew how busy you were."

A cold chill of anticipation passed through Randee, although she wouldn't have been able to give a logical reason why. "What kind of problems, Kimo?"

"Well, at first I just thought I was imagining things. On Monday, I checked the storeroom on board the boat, just like I do every week, you know, to figure out our weekly order. It seemed to me that some things were missing; a whole carton of the disposable cameras was gone and quite a bit of the liquor. So I rechecked the inventory sheets from last week's trips, and, sure enough, those things were there last week."

"So we've had some petty thievery." Randee pulled her hair back up on top of her head and secured it. She was determined not to let this minor problem destroy her good mood. "Okay, we'll change the locks. That's unfortunate, but it's not that big a problem, Kimo. We'll just be more careful in the future about who has access to the storeroom."

"I'm afraid there's more to it than that, Randee."

Randee noticed that Kimo's dark eyes betrayed a serious concern. "Tell me, Kimo."

Kimo cleared his throat, clearly uncomfortable. "Well, yesterday morning I went to the shop early to fill some extra tanks—we had six scuba divers going out on the morning cruise—and as soon as I unlocked, I noticed that brand-new set of gear, the one you bought last month, was gone."

"An entire set of new scuba gear?"

Kimo nodded sadly. "I'm afraid so."

Randee chewed her lip in frustration. "Was anything else taken from the shop?"

"Not that I could see. But today, when I came down to the

boat to do my regular safety check, I discovered that some of our extra life preservers are gone."

"What?" Randee's exasperation overflowed. "Liquor and scuba equipment and cameras I can understand. But why in the world would anyone want to steal life preservers?"

"I don't know. I just don't know. I'm terribly sorry, Randee." he hung his head in despair.

"It's not your fault, Kimo. Lord knows we could do without the extra expense of replacing that equipment, but we don't have a choice about that. But please, be extra careful for the next couple of days. Our first JTL passengers are on the manifest for Friday. I want everything to be perfect for them."

Late Friday morning, Cord stood on the tarmac and watched Jason take off with a full load of passengers. As the helicopter disappeared into the blue Kona sky, the cast on his leg felt heavier than ever, as if it were an anchor that would keep him earthbound forever. That thought, and the fact that he hadn't seen Randee since she'd been back from Honolulu, would be enough to put him in a foul temper for the rest of the morning.

Hell, even if he had seen her, it wouldn't have done any good. Just seeing her wouldn't have been enough to satisfy the raw ache he'd been living with since the very first day he'd met her.

The copter was now just a dot in the sky, and when Cord turned back he saw Randee stepping out of her van. She was wearing the practical shorts and T-shirt that were virtually her uniform when she was working at the *Kona Breeze* office, and her hair was pulled back in a sensible ponytail, but Cord thought she had never looked so beautiful. His gut wrenched with the realization of how much he had missed her. But as she came closer, it was clear that she was very upset about something. Her nose and cheeks were unnaturally red and her eyes were flashing green fire.

"Cord, I've got to talk to you right away." Her voice was unexpectedly abrupt.

"And a very pleasant good morning to you, too. How was your trip?"

"I'm sorry, Cord, I don't mean to be rude. The trip was great,

I'll tell you about it later. Right now I need to talk to you about something else. We've got a big problem."

"Okay. What's up?"

"I think someone's out to sabotage the *Kona Breeze.*"

"Sabotage? What the hell are you talking about?"

Randee quickly repeated what had happened while she was in Honolulu. Cord listened, waiting to hear what exactly had made her so excited. "Okay, so somebody stole some stuff. That ticks me off, too. But I don't understand what that has got to do with sabotage."

"It gets worse. This morning, while the boat was being prepped, one of the crew had a step collapse underneath him, just completely give way. Luckily, he only sprained his ankle." She brushed back a strand of hair that had fallen in her eyes and took a deep breath. "Cord, I looked at the ladder myself. No signs of wear at all. But all but one of the screws were missing."

"Are you saying someone deliberately loosened the step?"

"That's what it looked like to me. But that's not all. Today would have been our first day carrying passengers from one of the JTL tours."

"Would have been?" Cord was getting a bad feeling low in his gut.

"Yes. Except the boat wasn't able to go out this morning. The engines wouldn't start. Turned out the batteries were completely dead."

"Couldn't they be recharged?"

"Of course. Kimo couldn't find any reason for them to have gone dead, so he went right to work on getting them recharged, but—but—" She was fighting hard, but finally Randee's face began to crumple into tears. "I couldn't leave sixty-three Japanese tourists standing in the sun for two hours. I had to send them back to the hotel." She put her hand over her eyes to hide her tears. "Oh, Cord, sixty-three passengers! What am I going to tell the JTL people?"

Cord drew her carefully into his arms, and the tender gesture released a wave of racking sobs that betrayed the tension she had been living with over the past few weeks. He held her against him, and as she cried, he gently patted her back, comforting her like a small child, feeling the hurt and fear slowly drain out of her body.

Touching her this time felt different from the other times he had held her in his arms. Even though her body was soft and pliant against his, he did not feel the sudden surge of desire that had been there before. Instead, he was filled with the need to comfort her, to protect her. He hadn't felt that way about anyone in a very long time. Not since Brittany.

Finally, the crying stopped and Randee disentangled herself from his embrace. She searched for a tissue in her pocket and blew her nose.

"I'm sorry, Cord. I feel like such an idiot. I don't know what's wrong with me. I don't usually act this way."

"That's okay. I think maybe you just needed to have a good cry."

"Maybe." She blew her nose again and forced a smile. "In any case, there are things to be done. I need to call and make peace with the JTL office. Then I'm going to get to the bottom of this."

"How?" Cord didn't like the sound of this.

"I have a hunch that somebody from the inside is responsible for these problems. I already spend plenty of time in the office. I'm certain that there's nothing questionable going on there. But I need to get more involved with what's happening on board the boat. Until I know who's behind all these problems, I'll be keeping a very close eye on things. I'm going to join the crew of the *Kona Breeze*."

"You mean go out on the boat every day? Randee, I don't think that's such a great idea." The ache in his gut was getting worse, but he didn't want to upset Randee any more than she already was.

"Why not?" Randee crossed her arms defiantly. "I know my way around the boat."

"I'm sure you do, but I think you're dreaming up some kind of a plot that doesn't exist. I think you're letting your imagination get the best of you."

"But all these things, the stealing, the loose step, the dead batteries—"

"Are all probably just coincidences. I don't think you've got anything to gain by playing detective. Let the police handle the theft, and you stick to the business end of things." *And stay out of trouble,* he added silently. If there really was some kind of connection between these events, then the last place he wanted Randee was in the middle of it.

But before Randee spoke, the expression on her face told him his words had been wasted. "Cord, thank you for letting me cry on your shoulder, and I appreciate your advice, but this is my business. I'm not going to stand by and let it be destroyed in front of my eyes. I just can't do that. Tomorrow, when the *Kona Breeze* sets out for Kealakekua, I'll be on board."

"What's the status, Captain?" Randee gave her version of a smart salute, trying to inject some levity into what was a tense situation.

Kimo grunted into his coffee. "We're finally ready to board. I've been over every inch of this boat twice, and I can't find a thing out of place. Had to get up an hour earlier to do it, too." Kimo grunted again and took a last swig of coffee from his mug. "That lazybones Liko was supposed to help me, but he never got out of bed. I called him three times before I got disgusted and gave up."

Randee laughed. "Well, Kimo, if it's any comfort to you, I've yet to meet the father of a teenage boy who doesn't think his son's lazy at least sometimes."

"Maybe so, but Liko's not a boy anymore, he's eighteen. Time for him to start acting like a man, taking some responsibility for himself."

"I know you said he liked to work on the boat, but he's only been around a couple of times since I've been here. We could use the help, at least on weekends."

"I know. I'd like to have him on board myself. Why, when he was a little boy, he used to spend every afternoon after school and all day during the summer helping out. He was anxious to learn everything there was to know about the *Kona Breeze*. Got to be a pretty good sailor, too."

Kimo got up from his seat behind the wheel and scanned the empty horizon. "But then Mary Lei died, and well, in the last two years, he's been different. Not interested in much of anything."

"It's hard for a boy to lose his mother."

"Yes." Kimo slipped on his dark glasses. "And for a man to lose his woman." Randee's heart ached at the pain she heard in Kimo's voice. Kimo cleared his throat and continued more brightly.

"Anyway, Liko's no one's worry but mine. If you're ready, Randee, we'd better get started boarding and—hey, isn't that Cord?"

Randee spun around in time to see Cord walking, no *ambling* was more like it, down the dock. Something was odd about the sight. What was different? Of course! The obvious answer hit her in an instant. She ran to the lifelines that encircled the upper deck.

"Cord! Where are your crutches?"

He flashed her a thousand-watt grin that hit her like a blow to the stomach. "Don't need them anymore. This is what my doctor calls a walking cast." He indicated the new smaller cast that covered only the bottom half of his leg. "Pretty snazzy, huh?"

Randee rushed down the ladder, her knees a bit wobbly underneath her, to meet him as he boarded the boat. She was suddenly face-to-face with him. She took a tiny step back. Something about seeing him here like this, unexpectedly, had caught her seriously off guard. "That's great, I'm really happy for you, but what are you doing here?"

"I think it's about time for me to start contributing a little more to this partnership."

"What about Big Island Wings? What about Jason? Doesn't he need you?"

"Jason's got everything under control. The guy's a working machine. Actually, I'm really starting to feel like a fifth wheel over there, and I'm tired of feeling useless. So I thought that you could maybe use an extra hand out on the boat today, especially given the circumstances."

"Cord, that's very generous, but I don't know, with your cast—"

"Watch this." Cord scrambled up the steep ladder Randee had just descended and was on the upper deck in seconds. Randee followed him up.

"Well?" Cord stood defiantly, as if daring her to deny his obvious agility. But of course, the real reason she hesitated had noth-

ing to do with his leg. It had to do with the devastating effect he
had on her. If she thought that effect had been diffused, the last
few moments had proven her wrong. The *Kona Breeze* was a big
boat, but it wasn't big enough as far as Randee was concerned.
Not for both of them.

"Cord, I just don't know . . ."

"He gets around better than some of these wet-behind-the-ears
kids we got already, Randee," Kimo offered from his station behind the wheel. He glanced at his watch and then up at the morning sky. "We need to get going, or we'll be off schedule all day
long, and you know we've got a full boat today. Of course, it's
up to you, but we could sure use the help, if you ask me." Kimo
shrugged and tugged on the bill of his cap. "Besides, he's already
on the payroll, right? Might as well get some work out of him."

Cord grinned broadly. "Kimo's right, Randee. I'm here and
willing. You might as well be getting your money's worth out of
me." The sparkle in his eyes suggested endless, entirely inappropriate ways that she might do so.

Randee flushed and bit her lip, but she knew the battle was
already lost. She could tell from the good-natured but firm determination in Cord's eyes that there was no point in arguing with
him. It would have to be up to her to keep everything between
them on a strictly professional level. She could handle it; she
would have to.

"Okay. But please, be extra careful, especially when we're under way."

Cord took a step in close to her, and when he spoke, his voice
was pitched so softly that only she would hear him. "Don't worry.
I'll be careful; careful enough for both of us." His low, ragged
voice touched her like an intimate caress, and she shivered in
spite of the warm morning sun.

Randee swallowed, trying to ease the tightness she was feeling
in her throat. "Good. I wouldn't want anyone getting hurt."

His lips parted in a barely perceptible smile. "A very sensible
idea, Mrs. Turner. But unfortunately, no matter how careful we
are, sometimes accidents happen."

Nine

In spite of Randee's concerns, the next three days passed without incident. Ironically, they were among the best days for business that Randee could recall in the months since she had become owner of the *Kona Breeze*. The boat was filled to capacity for both the morning and afternoon cruises, and every trip passed without a hitch. Even Mother Nature cooperated, providing truly flawless weather: three days of crystal-clear skies, calm seas, and warm sunshine.

Their passengers had a wonderful time, and so the tour operators were happy. Even the marketing director of JTL, who had threatened to cancel her contract after the first ill-fated trip, had called to tell Randee how pleased he was with the reports he'd received on both Big Island Wings and the *Kona Breeze*.

Cord proved to be a great asset aboard the boat, efficient with his tasks and popular with the passengers. After the first day, even Kimo, who didn't give compliments lightly, told Randee that in spite of his cast, Cord was a first-class sailor, especially for a *haole*.

After she was convinced he wasn't going to fall overboard, Randee left Cord on his own on the boat. She told herself she simply wanted to keep an eye on all the other crew members, but the real reason was that when she was near him, she found it impossible to keep her eyes off his magnificent body, clad only in a brief pair of swim trunks and the plaster walking cast. It was a pleasure she was unable to resist, and Randee knew it wouldn't do much for her authority with the rest of the crew for them to catch her gawking at Cord like some lovesick adolescent, so she kept a careful distance.

Besides, she had more serious things on her mind. She'd meant what she'd told Cord about getting to the bottom of the mysterious events of the last week. She would not stand by and let her business be destroyed.

Yet her three days of vigilance had yielded nothing. In fact, things had never gone so smoothly. By the fourth day, Randee realized that in spite of her concerns, she had started to relax a bit. When the manifest for the afternoon trip showed a few openings, she impulsively called Auntie Lani to bring Rorey and join them for the afternoon cruise.

"Mama!" Randee looked up from her task of winding the forward lines to see Rorey walking along the dock, his hand firmly in Auntie Lani's grasp. She waved, her heart suddenly filled with joy at the sight of her son.

"Hi, baby! I'm right here!" Rorey waved back.

"He doesn't look like much of a baby to me." From nowhere, Cord appeared at her side. She didn't jump, for somehow she had sensed his presence before he even spoke. "Check out the outfit."

Randee had to admit, walking hand in hand with Auntie Lani, wearing his baseball cap and child-sized sunglasses, Rorey looked like an active little boy ready for a day of fun, and not like a baby at all. The realization pleased her, but the thought was not without a twinge of regret. "You're right. He's growing up. But he'll always be my baby."

Cord smiled indulgently at her. "Spoken like a true mother." Cord descended the stairway to the lower deck to help Lani and Rorey board. He reappeared moments later with Rorey in his arms and Lani close behind him.

"Here's the lady you're looking for, buddy." He gave Rorey to Randee and took Lani's enormous straw bag from her. "Here, Auntie Lani, I saved you the best spot, right here in front of the captain's station." Cord spread out her towel. "You and Rorey will be able to see everything from here."

"Ooo, Cord, you do know how to treat a girl!" Lani settled herself on the towel with surprising grace for her size. "Isn't that right, Randee?"

"Hmm," Randee answered with a noncommittal murmur. "We'd better get to work."

"We're ready to set sail, Randee." Kimo returned from his final check of the boat, ready to take his seat behind the wheel. "Cord, if you want to—" He stopped, suspended halfway between standing and sitting. "Lani?"

There was a long moment of silence before Lani answered, and when she spoke, her voice was uncharacteristically soft. "Yes. It's me, Kimo."

"Lani! My goodness, I haven't seen you in—" He settled heavily into his seat, a confused but pleased look on his face. "Gosh, I don't think . . . It must be . . ."

"A long time. A very long time, Kimo." Lani lowered her eyes to the deck and busied herself with straightening Rorey's cap. "Not since Mary Lei's service." She looked up, now gazing directly into the big man's eyes, and Randee felt as though the two of them had forgotten that she and Cord and a full boat of passengers surrounded them. "So how have you been getting along, Kimo?"

"I've managed, Lani. I've been getting along all right."

"That's the best we can expect, I suppose. Any of us." Lani looked around, as if suddenly aware of her surroundings again, and flashed a dazzling warm smile that now included the others. She laughed with nervous anticipation. "So, when does this little trip get under way?"

"Right now." Kimo fired up the engines to motor out of the harbor. "Cord, tell the boys to cast off."

Randee caught Cord's musing glance, but neither of them said anything. She could tell that Cord had also noticed the energy that was flowing between Kimo and Lani.

"Aye aye, Captain." Cord disappeared down the crew's ladder.

The sail to Kealakekua Bay was smooth and trouble-free, but with a full load of passengers there was still plenty of work for the crew to do. The hour-long trip was nearly over by the time Randee had a moment to check back on Lani and Rorey. As the *Kona Breeze* reduced its speed to enter the mouth of Kealakekua Bay, Randee climbed up to the top deck.

When she arrived at the captain's station, she found Kimo and Lani engrossed in conversation. Kimo said something in Hawaiian that Randee couldn't understand, and Lani laughed uproariously in response.

Rorey was nowhere to be seen. For an instant, panic surged through Randee's body.

"Where's Rorey?"

"Don't worry, Randee." Lani wiped tears from her eyes, barely holding back her laughter at Kimo's comments. "He's with Cord. He wanted to see the fish."

Randee felt relief flood through her. Inwardly, she chided herself for her maternal overreaction. As a single mother, Randee knew that she perhaps had even more than her share of natural protective instinct toward her child. She had never had the comfort of a partner whom she could count on to protect Rorey the way that she herself was compelled to. Maybe if she had, she wouldn't feel the almost paralyzing fears that overcame her from time to time.

She descended to the main deck, where passengers were gathered around the glass-bottom viewing windows. There she spotted Rorey, perched on the edge of the low wall that surrounded the glass bottom. Cord stood behind him, his arms wrapped securely around the boy's waist.

"Fishies!" Rorey pointed a chubby finger. "Fishies!"

"That's right. Lots of pretty fishies here, Rorey. Big ones, little ones." Cord didn't notice her approach but continued his quiet dialogue with her son. His attention was totally focused on Rorey. "That's a Moorish idol, and the little one over there the Hawaiians call the *humuhumunukuku'apua'a.* Isn't that a funny name? What a big name for a silly little fishy."

Something about the sight of Cord's strong, planed face near her son's chubby one moved her deeply. Randee stopped and just watched the two of them for a moment, man and boy together. She was suddenly overwhelmed with a tender sadness, a profound sense of grief over the loss that Rorey faced, a loss that he did not yet realize but that would affect him for the rest of his life. No matter how much she loved her son, she could never be a father to him. She could never fill that role, no matter how she tried. No mother on earth could do that.

"Mama!" Rorey had caught sight of her.

"Hi, boys." She cleared her throat, trying to keep the catch of emotion out of it. Cord would surely be confused by her reaction. "Checking out the fishies?" She joined them at the glass bottom.

"Mama, look!" Rorey pointed eagerly, leaning over as far as Cord's protective grasp would let him. "Fishies! Pretty fishies!"

"I see them, honey. Very pretty fishies." Randee forced herself to keep talking, her light tone belying her feelings. "How nice of Cord to show them to you. He even knows their names. He must know a lot about them."

Cord looked at her thoughtfully, as if reading her feelings. She had the odd sensation that somehow he was fully aware of the powerful emotions that now gripped her. "I'm no expert, Randee. I just know what I know." His voice was rough, and she wasn't sure if Cord was talking about the fish or the small boy he held in his arms.

"I'm not an expert either, Cord. I'm just doing the best that I can."

His eyes held hers. "That's all anybody can do, I guess."

The power blast of the ship's horn announcing their arrival broke the mood between them. "I guess I'd better help Kimo pick up the mooring." Cord handed Rorey over to her. "You stay with your mama for a while, buddy. We'll get a closer look at the fishies later."

Cord was true to his word, and Randee was delighted to see the two of them in a small inflatable dinghy floating on the calm, clear waters of Kealakekua Bay. To her surprise, Rorey, who had always been a bit nervous about the ocean, was completely relaxed with Cord, leaning over and splashing happily in the warm water as Cord held him securely.

As Randee watched the two of them float from her position on the stern of the *Kona Breeze*, she felt the sense of sorrow that had been with her begin to melt away. The warm sunshine, the gentle lapping of the water against the boat, and the happy laughter of her passengers both in and out of the water filled her with a sense of peace.

From time to time the voices of Auntie Lani and Kimo would drift down from the upper deck, where they were engrossed in catching up with one another's lives. As it turned out, the two were old friends; they had even attended the same schools as children but had lost touch over the last few years. It didn't escape Randee's notice that they both seemed exceptionally pleased to have found each other again.

The calm feeling stayed with her all day, and by the next morning when she was driving to Keauhou Bay, Randee had even started to wonder if perhaps Cord had been right, if everything that had happened aboard the *Kona Breeze* during her absence had merely been unrelated incidents; inconvenient, expensive, and annoying, but nothing more sinister than that.

She turned into the parking lot and found a space next to Cord's beat-up old Jeep. Now that he had his walking cast, he was able to manage driving without too much trouble, although flying was still out of the question. But now that they had Jason, Cord seemed less anxious about returning to the pilot's seat.

As Randee locked up her van, she noticed that Cord and Kimo were on the dock, but the equipment carts that they usually used to load supplies were nowhere in sight. That was surprising. Surely they weren't finished already; it was much too early. As she started across the parking lot, Randee began to sense that something wasn't as it should be. Kimo, who always preferred to sit rather than stand whenever he had a choice, was nervously walking up and down the dock, as if he were preparing to walk the plank of a pirate ship.

Cord stood on the dock near the stern of the boat, completely still, arms folded across his chest. Even from the distance of the parking lot, Randee could read the tension that radiated from Cord's body. A sudden feeling of dread washed over her like an icy wave. She suddenly knew with sickening certainty that something was wrong. Terribly wrong.

She started walking fast, then unable to endure the tension of waiting a moment longer, she dropped her purse and broke into a run. Seconds later, she was on the dock. Cord turned toward her, but his face was a stony mask she couldn't read.

"Oh, Randee, I am so sorry." Kimo rushed to meet her, looking almost as if he were about to cry. "I am so terribly sorry." Randee looked beyond the two men to where the boat was waiting on its lines. For a moment she froze, unable to move, and all of a sudden she was afraid she would vomit.

Broad stripes of ugly black spray paint crisscrossed the interior of the cabin like the web of some enormous venomous spider. The royal blue seat cushions were slashed to ragged shreds, and the foam stuffing was scattered about the deck like dirty snow.

Crude symbols whose meaning she could not interpret covered the smooth white walls.

For a moment Randee could not move or speak. Then she gathered her resolve and stepped onto the boat, hot tears of anger and frustration forming behind her eyes, but she would not let them come. She walked carefully among the debris, unable to believe the senseless destruction that surrounded her. Her head was pounding with a pulse that matched the quickened beating of her heart.

Feeling as if she might faint, Randee sat down on one of the benches running the length of the lower cabin. She was dimly aware of Cord boarding the boat and climbing to the upper deck, and she wanted to call out to him, but she was too miserable to even speak. She heard him moving about on the deck above her. Her head sagged, and she buried her face in her hands. Shock, anger, sorrow, and despair chased one another within her, like ill-behaved dogs.

After what felt like hours, Randee felt a solid arm encircle her shoulders. Without even opening her eyes, she let Cord enfold her against his solid chest. She let herself enjoy the comfort and warmth of his body for several minutes, allowing his strength to support her. Finally, when she knew she could wait no longer, she pulled herself free to look him straight in the eye.

"How bad is it?" She needed to face the truth. There was no point in hiding, she knew that, even though right now she wished she could just disappear.

"Not nearly as bad as it looks." Cord gave her a grim smile. "And it looks pretty bad, I know. But believe it or not, we actually got off lucky this time." He gestured roughly at the destruction around them. "Randee, I know this all looks terrible, but it's just petty vandalism, ugly but superficial. The bastards could have done some real serious damage to the navigational instruments, or to the engine, that would have put us out of commission for a long time. But they didn't; I've looked at those systems and everything checks out fine."

"Then why? What's the point?" Randee felt confusion wash over her in waves. "Why would anyone do this to the *Kona Breeze?*"

"I'm not sure why, exactly, but I have a hunch that whoever

did this just wants to intimidate you." He reached for her and gently cradled her face between his massive hands. The warmth felt good against her damp cheeks. "But it's not going to work, is it, Randee? You're not going to let this thing get to you, are you?"

"Oh, Cord. I'm trying. I really am. I just feel sick. I want to go home and go to bed and pull the covers over my head and die."

"We're going to get through this, together." His hands dropped to her shoulders. "The rest of the crew will be here soon. Let's not spook them, if we can help it. There will be enough gossip around town the way it is. If we get the whole crew started right away, I think we can get everything cleaned up by tomorrow morning. We'll let Kimo handle the questions and the refunds for those folks." Cord jerked his thumb in the direction of the group of tourists who were already gathering in the parking lot for the morning cruise.

"What are we going to do? What if something like this happens again?" Randee heard her own words as if they were being spoken by someone else. "Or something worse? Cord, I don't know what—"

"I'll make sure nothing happens." Cord's voice was like tempered steel, smooth and cold and strong.

"What do you mean? How?"

"I'm spending the night here tonight."

"Here? On the boat?"

"Yes. Right here on the *Kona Breeze*. That way, any bastard who wants to screw around with this boat is going to have to get by me first." Somehow, without speaking any louder, an element of menace entered Cord's voice, a dark note that sent a shiver up Randee's backbone. She felt with certainty that anyone who crossed Cord would most certainly regret having done so. Even so, what might happen to Cord in the process? The damage done to the *Kona Breeze* might be only a warning of what the vandals were capable of doing. Her fear over the future of the boat was now far overshadowed by her concern for Cord.

"Cord, I appreciate your offer, I really do, but I can't let you do that. The *Kona Breeze* is my problem, and besides, you've still got your cast on. It's out of the question. You could get hurt, alone out here at night. Anything could happen. I won't let you put yourself in danger because of me."

"It's not quite that simple, Randee. You seem to be forgetting that I also have a vested interest in this situation. We have a partnership."

"But it's just not safe." Randee could feel herself losing this argument already. "We don't know who we're dealing with here. What if something should happen to you?"

Cord smiled, but it was a small, tight smile that was without humor.

"Believe me, Randee, I know how to take care of myself." He took both her hands in his and squeezed them with a gentle, firm pressure that underscored each word.

"I'm staying here tonight, and every night, until I find out who's responsible for this." He released her hands and stood up. He turned to examine a splash of dark paint on the wall of the cabin, rubbing at it with his thumb, first gently, then harder and harder. Finally he stopped and turned back to Randee.

"But now it's time for us to get to work."

Ten

The sun had already slipped below the horizon, but the deep rose afterglow of the sunset was still washed across the sky when Cord pulled his Jeep into the parking lot. He got out carefully, still conscious of his nearly healed leg, and hoisted his backpack out from behind his seat. Before slamming the door, he slowly surveyed the parking lot, looking for anything out of the ordinary. Nothing appeared out of place. The sales office was locked up tight, and at the dock the boat was drifting serenely on its lines.

Cord boarded the *Kona Breeze* and climbed to the upper deck, figuring it would be the best place from which to hold his watch. He dropped his backpack and settled into the captain's chair behind the wheel. He turned the chair slowly around, a full three hundred sixty-degree turn. His gaze passed over the parking lot and dock, then the small sandy beach adjacent to it, then over the palm trees that covered the point, and finally to the mouth of the bay and the open ocean.

The sight of the sea usually calmed him, soothed his spirit when he'd spent too much time thinking, too much time remembering things that were better left in the past. There wasn't much in his past that was pleasant to remember; and he considered the future an unknown journey, not to be feared, but not to be trusted, either. Better, he'd always thought, much better to live in the present. Enjoy the glories of life in this island paradise, the simple pleasures of the here-and-now, depend only on yourself, and don't waste time on a lot of fancy plans for tomorrow.

That philosophy had worked for him, well enough anyway, for nearly ten years now. And if he hadn't been exactly happy, well, at least he hadn't made anybody else miserable in the process.

He never wanted to do to another what had been done to him. So being independent, accountable to no one, responsible for no one, caring for no one—that had been his way. It was Brittany's legacy to him.

But two events had turned his simple philosophy upside down, inside out, and backwards. The first was the accident. The second was meeting Randee Turner. From the first event, he would soon be recovered, physically, anyway; just as good as new, at least that's what the doctors said. But from the second, he wasn't so sure.

From their very first meeting, she'd been disrupting his world, challenging him, daring him. She wasn't put off by the same prickly defenses that had kept most of his world at a safe distance. Sure, he'd thought he'd had her pegged right from the start, known what she was about, what box she fit into. But he'd been wrong.

And now, here he was. Alone on the water at night, keeping watch for who or what he didn't know, trying to protect—what, a boat? A business? No, that was only part of it. In a strange way, he knew what he was here for. He was here because he wanted to protect Randee.

He remembered the night they had stood together in this same spot, watching the sun disappear. How sweet her mouth had been that night, like warm spiced honey. His hands ached with the memory of her body, ached to feel the silken smoothness of her breasts, to feel her nipples peak and pucker with pleasure under his fingers. The thought brought a heavy ache to his groin. *Better derail this train of thought, old buddy.* Cord shifted uncomfortably in his seat. *There's no relief in it; not tonight, not ever.*

A sound behind him caught his attention. Cord spun around, his fantasy evaporating, as each of his senses became instantly alert and focused. Something moved in the shadow just beyond the ring of light at the foot of the dock.

At that moment, Cord thought his earlier imaginings had taken on solid form. A woman appeared in the circle of light, a wicker basket on her arm. She paused, looking toward the boat, straining to see.

"Don't shoot. It's only me."

"Randee! What are you doing here?" Cord scrambled to the edge of the upper deck.

"Stay there, I'm coming up." She climbed the ladder.

"I sure didn't expect to see you here tonight."

"I didn't know I was coming, either, until just a few minutes ago." She held the wicker basket in front of her, both hands wrapped around the handle. Tucked under her arm was a small folded blanket. She was wearing white cotton pants and a brightly colored tropical print blouse. Her face glowed with color from the last few days out on the water.

They stood in silence for a long moment before Cord spoke. "So why *are* you here, Randee?" If his imagination had been driving him crazy, having her here in person was far worse. She was too close, too real to ignore.

"Auntie Lani sent this." She extended the basket. "If you're going to be out here alone all night, she said you deserve a decent meal. You know how she is; sometimes I think she believes all the world's problems could be solved by a good hot meal."

"She's really something."

"You're right about that." Randee put the basket down on the deck and knelt down beside it. "I took a peek while I was in the car. It looks delicious."

Cord watched in silence as Randee spread out the red plaid blanket. She opened the basket and withdrew a bottle of wine and a corkscrew. "So do you want to do the honors with this, or should I?"

"I'll take care of it." Cord sat down on the blanket and went to work on the cork. "Looks like Auntie Lani—" He tugged harder on the corkscrew. "—Has really gone all out." The cork popped out with a satisfying sound.

"Well, she appreciates what you're doing for me." Randee held out two glasses for him to fill. After he poured, she kept one for herself and passed the other to him. "And so do I." She clinked her glass on his.

"We're partners. Right?"

"Right." Randee took a sip from her wineglass but continued to watch Cord over the rim. He was sitting cross-legged on the blanket, looking out over the dark water of the bay. What was he thinking right now? He was a difficult man to read, even for someone as intuitive as she was. In spite of their partnership, in spite of the time they had spent together, she knew practically nothing about him, about his past, about his life. As guarded as Cord was, she could probably be his partner until they were both old and gray and not know any more than she knew right now.

Randee was determined to change that. Cord's insistence on staying on board the boat had moved her far more than she had allowed him to see. She wanted to know more about this man.

"Let's see what Auntie Lani made for us." Randee reached into the basket. She began to unpack plates, silverware, and various containers. She peeled open the lid of one and a puff of fragrant steam wafted out. "Mm, her specialty!"

"Laulau chicken?"

"That's right. Remember, that's what she was making the night you were supposed to come to dinner and . . ." Randee's voice trailed off.

"Yes, I remember." His tone told Randee that Cord remembered that night just as well as she did. The first time he'd touched her. The first time he'd kissed her.

"Let's eat before this gets cold." Randee served the chicken and opened the other containers of rice and vegetables. They ate in silence for a while, enjoying the delicious food and balmy night.

"More wine?" Cord tipped the bottle toward her. Randee lifted her glass and let him fill it, then his own. Relaxed by the wine, Randee was determined to try to fill in some of the blanks that surrounded her partner.

"This is the kind of night that makes you remember that we live in paradise." Randee looked up at the stars. "Nowhere else in the world is quite like this."

"You're right about that. I haven't been back to the mainland for nearly fifteen years."

"Is your family here in the islands?"

"No."

Randee waited for him to elaborate, but he didn't continue. She decided not to let the subject drop. "So where is your family from? Where did you grow up?"

"L.A. But the only family I ever had was my mother, and she died when I was fourteen."

"That must have been hard."

Cord shrugged. "Mom did the best she could, but I was kind of a wild kid. Money was really tight, so we lived in a pretty rough neighborhood, and I found a lot of ways to get into trouble. It was right before she died that I started getting into trouble with the law."

"What kind of trouble?"

"Kid stuff, mostly. But some friends of mine decided to help themselves to somebody else's car for the night, and I went along for the ride. We got caught." Cord's voice was matter-of-fact, neither apologizing nor seeking sympathy. "Then Mom died and I ended up in Juvenile Hall. I was in and out of there twice, but when they let me out the last time I was placed with a foster family that treated me pretty well. I lived with them for two years and got straightened out. My foster father had been in the military and so I went into the Marine Corps as soon as I was old enough."

Randee made some quick mental calculations. "That must have been during Vietnam." Randee formed a picture of Cord in her mind as a confused young man, hurting and trying to put some order in his life. The image made her heart ache for that long-ago boy.

"Yeah, that was when things were pretty hot over there. But I didn't care. Believe it or not, at that point in my life, dying didn't seem like something that terrible." There was a long silence, and Cord's eyes were distant with memory. "But I was wrong. Death is terrible, and I saw a whole lot of it, more than most. I lost count of all the flights I made where most of my passengers were in body bags, or would be soon." He shook his head, very slowly, his mouth a hard line.

His words called up images of death in her mind, images Randee was anxious to push away. She shook her head and let the shiver run through her before she spoke again.

"But that was when you learned to fly."

Cord's expression lifted, and he met Randee's eyes. "Yes. And that was wonderful. The flying part of it, I mean. That's what made me realize that I *didn't* want to die." Cord's eyes were bright with emotion. "When I was free, free in the sky, that's when I knew that I wanted to live, damn it! And that's when I knew that if I survived, I would make a whole new life, a new life flying where the sky was peaceful and my passengers were laughing and happy." His voice trailed off. "Instead of sick, or dying, or dead."

Cord swallowed the last of his wine in a single gulp and put down the glass. Randee quietly cleared away the remains of their meal. She slipped everything into the picnic basket and closed the lid. Cord was staring out at the sea, beyond the mouth of the bay, beyond where the waves were breaking. His eyes were distant and filled with memories that she could only guess at.

Randee put the picnic basket aside and moved close to Cord, her own eyes following the trajectory of his gaze, trying to see what he was seeing, although she knew it only existed in his mind's eye. She wished that she could wipe away the memories that still weighed him down.

Randee sat up on her knees and reached for his face, bringing her lips to meet his in a gentle kiss, a kiss of comfort and understanding. For just a moment, they stayed like that, lips pressed together, Randee's small hands framing Cord's face. Then she felt the spark. The flame was there again, the heat that was always present when they were alone together, just below the surface.

Randee's lips parted, and their kiss deepened into passion. Slowly, Cord began to explore her mouth with his tongue. His arms encircled her, then carefully lifted her onto his lap, never breaking contact from her mouth. She began to feel a warm glow in her chest growing as Cord held her tight against his solid body.

Gently, Cord broke the kiss, his lips lingering over her mouth, reluctant to lose contact. He pulled back, and his eyes were dark with emotion. He studied her face, and she knew that something was troubling him.

"Randee, I want you to tell me the truth."

"The truth about what?" Her heart was still pounding with desire, a desire that she knew Cord shared—his body was making that perfectly clear. Yet he was stopping.

"I would like you to tell me what really happened between you and your husband."

Her insides twisted. "You know I'm a widow."

"I also know you haven't told me the whole truth. I could sense that there was more to the story than what you told me. I was certain of that from the very beginning."

The familiar burst of hot pain exploded in her chest. She didn't want to tell Cord. She didn't want to have to remember the pain of those years.

"Cord, I don't—"

Cord took her hand into both of his, and the concern she saw in his eyes told her she must share those things she did not want to share, talk about the memories she'd just as soon leave long buried. He deserved to hear it all.

"You're right, Cord. I haven't told you everything." Randee took a deep breath. "But I will." Without thought, Randee leaned her head against Cord's shoulder, looking out toward the dark water. His hand stroked her hair gently, encouraging her.

She started softly, trying to tell the story with as few words as possible. But as the whole truth came pouring out, she found that she no longer had control of her voice. She told Cord everything. She told him of her dreams when she first met and fell in love with Max Turner. She told him of her despair when she felt things between them begin to change.

"But what about Rorey? What happened when you got pregnant?" Cord's voice was gruff, but Randee could sense the concern beneath it. The image of Cord floating in the water with her son, pointing out the fish, and talking gently to him flashed into her mind.

"I didn't tell him."

"What?"

"I mean not at first. I was going to, but—" Randee swallowed hard, fighting the gorge of emotion that was rising in her throat. She took a deep breath. "I went to the doctor first. I wanted to be certain before I told Max. When the doctor confirmed it, I planned on telling him that night, when he got home from his office." She swallowed again, unable to keep back her tears any longer. "Cord, I so wanted things to be all right again. But then he never came home."

"What do you mean?"

"Not that night. I waited up all night. I was sick with worry, afraid he'd been in an accident or Lord knows what. He finally showed up about eight the next morning. He was wearing the same clothes he'd left the house in, and looked a little rumpled, but otherwise he seemed fine."

Cord took her hand, as if he sensed her need for encouragement. "Go on."

"I grabbed him and hugged him. I think I was crying; I was just so relieved that he was all right. But I could tell the instant

I touched him that something was wrong." Randee stopped for just a moment, feeling herself traveling vividly back to the scene she was recalling. "He didn't hug me back. He didn't even speak. That was when I knew."

"What?"

"That he'd been with someone else. Another woman. I could smell her on him, her perfume, her body!" Randee shook her head. "He didn't say a word. Just went upstairs and took a shower, as if nothing had happened."

"But, Randee, how could you be so sure?"

"I knew, Cord. I just knew. But you're right, I had to be absolutely sure. So I didn't tell him about the baby, and I started watching him in a new way." She shook her head again and heard herself almost laugh, a bitter sound of disillusionment. "I don't know how I could have been so blind, so stupid!" Cord took both her hands in his and held them tight. The strength of his hands comforted her and helped her continue.

"There were signs everywhere. I just had never noticed before; it had simply never crossed my mind. The late nights at the office, missed dinners, sudden trips out of town. Little things like matches from restaurants I'd never been to; strange phone calls late at night." She smiled, a tight line with no pleasure in it. "I even found lipstick-stained cigarettes in the ashtray of his car. The ultimate cliché, right?"

"The bastard." Cord's voice was soft but tinged with dark menace.

"So you see, it wasn't just once. It wasn't even just one woman. Max had been seeing other women from the day we'd gotten back from our honeymoon."

"My God, Randee. What did you do?"

"Nothing. I didn't say anything. I finally told him about the baby, when I couldn't hide it any longer. He seemed thrilled, and I hoped that maybe the baby would change him, bring him back to me."

"And?" Cord's voice was like a knife.

"I was a fool. After Rorey was born, he became even more blatant, almost as if he *wanted* me to confront him. And so finally I did."

"What did he say?"

"He laughed. Laughed as if I'd finally gotten some colossal joke, some nasty practical joke that he'd been waiting for me to fall into. He said, 'We have an arrangement, my dear Randee. Think of it as a business deal, if you like. That's something you can understand. And in this deal, we each get what we want. I don't intend to change a thing.' "

Cord put his arms around her and held her, the two of them rocking back and forth with an almost imperceptible motion. "That was when I moved out. I couldn't stay, not after that. Everything had been a lie. Everything." Randee stayed silent for a few minutes, letting the soothing motion of the boat and Cord's body calm her. When she spoke again, she was surprised at how composed her voice sounded.

"He was dead less than a month later. Car accident, just him, thank God, no other cars involved. The police said he was legally drunk. He was coming home from a hotel, where he'd been—been *with* a woman. A woman I knew. Actually, she was the wife of the man who was Max's best man at our wedding."

Now the flood of pain had passed its peak and slowed back down to silence. Cord began to kiss her face gently, kisses of comfort and understanding, devoid of insistence or demand, kisses that gently brushed away the tears she had not even realized she'd been shedding.

"And what happened to all his money? I thought the bastard was some hotshot tycoon. Shouldn't you and Rorey have been set for life?"

In spite of her pain, Randee couldn't help smiling. "So I guess you've finally figured out I'm not exactly a wealthy widow?"

"Yeah, I figured that out some time ago." Randee could hear the chagrin in his voice.

"And I thought I was doing such a good job playing the wealthy benefactor."

"Look, Randee, I'm sorry that I was such a jerk about all that."

"That's okay. Everybody else pretty much thought the same thing, I'm afraid. Actually, Max did have a great many assets; unfortunately, it was pretty much a house of cards. He'd inherited a substantial amount of money from his family, but despite his brilliant reputation and his family name, he just wasn't a good businessman."

"Was he dishonest?"

Randee shrugged. "At least sometimes. Nobody knows for sure. But his ego was much too big for him to take advice from anyone else, and so he made a lot of foolish mistakes. He'd usually been able to cover them up with some new complicated deal, but once he was dead, everything simply fell apart." She paused for a moment. Beside her, Cord was silent, but she could feel his unspoken encouragement to share everything.

"And of course, he'd always liked to spend money, whether he could really afford it or not. Every property he owned was mortgaged to the hilt, not to mention all the unpaid taxes that had accumulated. He'd sucked every business he owned dry, just bled every dime out of it."

"Including Paradise Fragrances?"

"Yes. Including Paradise Fragrances. When the estate was finally settled, properties sold and debts settled, all I got was the *Kona Breeze*. That and my jewelry were all that was left. Max bought the *Kona Breeze* as part of a big land development deal he was doing with Jack Haster. He'd never intended to keep it— probably never even saw it. The simple truth is that he hadn't owned it long enough to destroy it."

They sat in silence for several long minutes. Randee let herself completely relax, her body totally supported by Cord. Her breathing fell into the same slow pattern that she could feel in the rise and fall of his chest. She closed her eyes and let that primal rhythm and the gentle rocking of the boat lull her into a delicious half-sleep that she felt she could drift in forever.

As she drifted in the solid comfort of Cord's arms, Randee felt an odd lightness growing within her. The familiar ache that always surrounded her heart when she let herself think about the past was gone. Somehow, telling Cord the whole story had been freeing, even uplifting. A sudden burst of realization hit Randee. At this moment, she felt a tremendous sense of freedom, a feeling that she hadn't experienced since coming to the Big Island. And somehow, instead of the pain and depression she'd expected, there had been a feeling of comfort and liberation in sharing her story with Cord. His total acceptance of her had transformed her hurt.

Now it was her turn to give to him. Her mouth found his, and this time their kiss was one of heat, of need, of desire. She shifted on his lap, and her hands began to explore the body that had held her so tenderly. Cord moaned in response to her searching fingers, and the dark ragged sound sent a shiver of corresponding need and anticipation vibrating through her very center.

She kissed him again, hard and passionately, and beneath her thighs she felt his body surge and swell in response. With his body's needs so apparent, Randee felt a tremendous sense of her own feminine power that thrilled her. The knowledge that Cord wanted her, that he *needed* her, intensified her own desire like gasoline thrown on a fire.

Randee was fired with the sudden exquisite awareness that she wanted Cord to make love to her. Her caresses became more bold, more unrestrained. She longed to experience all of him. She wanted him to be lost in her and she in him, right here, right now, with the warm tropical air caressing their naked bodies.

An unexpected noise jerked Randee from her fantasy. Her eyes met Cord's, and she could see that he had become instantly alert, every inch of his body straining to listen. They sat motionless for a moment, each of them intent on listening. Then, unmistakably, the sound was there again. Cord put a warning finger to his lips, and Randee felt her heart beating hard within her chest.

A heavy shuffling sound, then something dragging. Footsteps. Someone was approaching, walking down the long, dark dock that led to the *Kona Breeze*.

Eleven

Cord eased Randee off his lap slowly, moving her to the deck without a sound. Her eyes searched his face for direction. He motioned to her to be quiet and to lie down flat on the deck, out of sight behind the captain's station. She nodded her understanding, then disappeared to her hiding place, moving with silent grace.

Cord ignored the sweat that was now trickling down his forehead. Keeping low, he moved quickly and soundlessly to the edge of the deck, being careful to keep the foot of his walking cast from striking the fiberglass floor too hard. He needed to keep the advantage of surprise.

He peered over the edge of the deck toward the ring of light where the shadowy dock met the dark parking lot. A figure had just slipped out of the light into the long, dark passage of the dark. Whoever it was had a heavy tread and was moving slowly but steadily down the dock.

Cord considered his choice of the broad passenger staircase or the steep crew's ladder. Although it would be tougher to navigate silently, he opted for the ladder, which was concealed in the shadows on the side of the boat that faced the mouth of the bay. The hulking figure was now nearly halfway down the dock.

Cord made his choice and moved to the ladder. Silently cursing his cast, he made his way down the ladder. On the last step, he misjudged the distance and kicked the metal riser with a sharp bang. He froze on the ladder, breath held, waiting, listening for a response. The footsteps stopped for a moment. Cord counted ten beats of his heart, then the footsteps started again.

Cord stepped off the ladder into the shadows of the interior lower deck. Now in the darkness he was moving mostly by memory, and he prayed that the afternoon cleanup crew had stowed everything in its approved place. Luckily, everything was as it should be, and he made it to the opposite side of the cabin without mishap.

His hands explored the starboard wall near the utility closet, and his fingers closed around the fireman's ax that was securely bracketed to the wall. His searching fingers found the bracket releases, and in a moment he had the heavy ax in his hands.

He moved swiftly to the deeply shadowed corner adjacent to the boarding area as the figure prepared to step through onto the boat. Cord waited until the last possible second, then stepped out of the darkness onto the open stern, ax suspended in the air menacingly.

"Step onto this boat and I'll split your skull."

"Cord, no! It's me, Kimo!" The familiar voice was shaky with fear.

"Kimo! My God!" Randee couldn't contain the relief that flooded through her. She left her position behind the captain's station and scrambled down the ladder, nearly losing her footing twice, her arms and legs tingling from being pressed against the hard surface of the deck. She fumbled around for nearly a minute before she found the electrical panel and snapped on the overhead lights.

The sudden glare revealed Kimo on the dock, obviously terrified, his eyes glued to Cord and the ax he still held warily in his hands. A large green duffel bag was on the ground at his side.

"Kimo, you scared us to death!" Randee's mind was racing, trying to process the barrage of information that was assaulting her. "What are you doing here? It's after midnight." Randee moved closer to Cord.

"I—I'm sorry I scared you. I couldn't sleep, I was so worried about the boat. I thought I would come down and keep Cord company." Kimo looked at Randee and dropped his eyes, stuttering in embarrassment. "I—I guess he's got enough company already."

Randee felt her cheeks aflame, but this was hardly a time to worry about propriety. She put her hand on Cord's arm. "Cord, it's okay. Please put that thing down." She tried to catch his eye, to seek some reassurance there, but Cord was still completely focused on Kimo. "Cord, please."

With obvious reluctance, Cord let the ax drop to his side but did not return it to the wall bracket from which he'd pulled it.

"Come on, Kimo." Randee motioned the big man aboard. "I'm sorry for the misunderstanding, but with everything that's been going on around here lately, I guess we're all a little bit on edge."

"No, I'm the one who's sorry, Randee. I should have realized that—that—I was just so worried, I just didn't think, that's all. There's no excuse." He sat down on the step, visibly shaken. He buried his head in his hands. "I'm so sorry. I can't seem to do anything right, lately."

"It's all right, Kimo." Randee looked at Cord, wishing he would reassure Kimo as well, but he remained silent. "It was just a mistake, that's all. Now why don't you calm down and go home. You need to get some sleep. We've got a full boat tomorrow."

"I guess you're right." Kimo turned to Cord. "I'm awfully sorry, Cord, really I am." Cord just nodded, and Kimo stepped back off the boat. He picked up his canvas duffel. "I guess I'll see the two of you tomorrow." The big man turned and walked back toward the parking lot, shaking his head and muttering under his breath.

When he was out of sight, Randee ran her hand up Cord's arm. "Well, that was a relief. I was scared to death until I saw it was only Kimo."

Cord stood for a moment, watching the empty dock. "Yes, I guess you're probably right." He returned the ax to its bracket. "But I'm not so sure . . ."

"Cord, what do you mean? Are you suggesting that Kimo could actually have something to do with what's been going on around here?"

"I don't know. But I'm not sure I buy his story of coming down here to keep me company. The whole thing sounds pretty fishy to me."

"Cord, I know it might seem suspicious to you, but Kimo is the last person in the world who would ever do anything to hurt the *Kona Breeze*. He thinks of her as his own, like a part of his family. You saw how upset he was the morning we discovered the vandalism. And tonight he was so distraught he could barely talk!"

"You're right about that."

"Kimo has worked on this boat since he was a teenager. I think he told me it will be twenty years this coming October that Jack Haster hired him as a deckhand. And he's been captain now for the last fifteen years." Randee captured one of Cord's big hands between both of her small ones. "He even gets his family involved when we're busy. His son, Liko, practically grew up on the boat, from what Kimo says."

"So you're not suspicious?"

"No, not at all." Randee could tell Cord was not convinced, but to her relief, he seemed content to let the subject drop. She was suddenly aware that she was still holding on to Cord's hand. She squeezed it once, then released him.

The sensual mood that had been burning and growing between them since she'd brought dinner had been shattered by Kimo's arrival, and in its wake was merely an awkward silence that hung between them like a dense morning fog. Randee suddenly felt very tired, and inexplicably melancholy, as though she'd lost something important and might never find it again.

"Well, I guess I should be getting home." She made no move to leave.

"Are you sure?" Cord's blue eyes were clouded with an emotion that she was having trouble reading.

"I don't want to worry Auntie Lani." Randee forced a smile. "Sometimes I'm afraid she thinks I need a baby-sitter as much as Rorey does."

"Be sure and tell her thank you from me for dinner." He smiled crookedly, and Randee felt the mood lift a bit. "I certainly can't remember when I've had anything quite as, well, delicious."

"Yes." Randee felt a shiver of heightened awareness pass through her. "Yes, she's quite the cook."

Cord kissed her once, quickly this time, with only a brief hint of the taste that had been driving her mad. "Be careful going home."

"I will." Randee picked up the basket and stepped onto the dock. "I'll see you in the morning." She walked down the dock quickly and was nearly running by the time she reached the parking lot.

Cord watched Randee pass through the lighted circle at the

base of the dock, and then into the darkness of the parking lot. He waited for the sound of her van. He heard it jump into life, and a second or two later the headlights cut the darkness. He stood and watched as the van turned around and kept watching until it disappeared out of sight.

For several long minutes he stood there in silence, looking toward the narrow road she'd taken into the tropical night. Then he retrieved the ax from its place on the wall and climbed the stairs back to the upper deck to continue his watch.

Cord slumped down in the captain's chair and put his feet up on the wheel. Although he wasn't sleepy, he pulled out the thermos of coffee that he had brought with him from home and poured himself a cup. He stared out to sea and sipped at the steaming, bitter brew without tasting it.

Cord tried to force his mind to work on the problem of the recent attacks against the *Kona Breeze*, but he was having trouble concentrating and he could feel the beginning of a headache forming behind his eyes. He put down his coffee and rubbed the bridge of his nose between his thumb and forefinger, and as he did so, he caught the slight fragrance of Randee's skin that still lingered on his fingers. He indulged himself in inhaling the bit of fragrance that remained on his hand. He didn't know the name of the perfume, had never smelled anything else like it, but that bare essence of sweetness released a torrent of sensual images in his mind.

He shook his head and picked up the plastic cup of coffee and drank. He inhaled the hot, bitter smell deeply into his lungs, trying to drive out what remained of Randee's sweet fragrance. But even when the scent was gone, the memories remained, as vivid as fresh paint on a canvas. And already he knew that no matter what happened, he would not be able to drive them from his mind. They had become a part of him now, burned into his very being.

Cord spent the next six nights on the *Kona Breeze*, but never again did he let Randee stay with him. When she tried to insist, he told her it was for her own safety, that he didn't want her getting in the way of what would be a very nasty scene. Finally, she acquiesced, but her eyes were full of unspoken hurt that tore at Cord's heart.

But the truth had little to do with Randee's safety. There was only one real reason Cord didn't want Randee alone with him on the boat; he knew his control could not last for another night like the one that had been interrupted by Kimo's arrival. His desire for Randee was growing stronger with each day, and that was trouble.

Of course he wanted to make love to her. There was no point in pretending that it wasn't so. He wanted her with a fierce, hot need, a need that demanded to be satisfied, and yet he knew that he must not dare to let himself taste the full pleasure of her body.

Cord was afraid. Afraid of what he was starting to feel for Randee. Afraid that his desire would never be satisfied in one night, or even a dozen nights. He knew that this desire would lead only to pain, a pain he had vowed to never open himself to again. He knew about desire, and he knew about pain. He had let himself love a woman before, completely and without restraint, and that had nearly destroyed him. He wouldn't be foolish enough to let that happen again.

Randee parked the van in her regular space facing the calm water of Keauhou Bay. She could see Cord standing on the upper deck of the boat, his morning cup of coffee in hand, staring out to sea. The morning breeze stirred his hair, which gleamed bright in the sunlight.

For a week of mornings she had found him in the same position, apparently still awake from his night watch. If he ever slept, she didn't know when it was, because he was still spending his days out on the boat. Other than the faint dark circles beneath his eyes, he seemed unaffected by his sleepless nights. At sea, he still outperformed all the regular crew members at their jobs as he had done from the very beginning. When Randee suggested that he take a day off and rest, he flatly refused. And after all, they did need the help—the *Kona Breeze* had been at capacity for the whole week.

But things had changed between them. Randee had felt the difference from their first moment together the morning after their picnic on the boat. Cord seemed to have withdrawn from her. He was polite, yes, almost too much so. But he was cool and distant, making their relationship as businesslike as possible. And now every polite, civilized interchange ripped her like a knife.

Randee longed for the raw honesty that they had shared that night on the boat, for the satisfaction of finally letting go of the painful secrets that each of them carried. She hungered for that feeling even more than she longed to taste the warmth of his mouth on hers again, to feel the strength of his body against hers once more.

To Randee's sorrow, they did not speak of what had happened, and what had almost happened, between them that night, not even obliquely. It was as if Cord wanted to erase everything that had passed between them that night, both the secrets they had shared as well as the intimate touches. His silence cut her far worse than any harsh words might have, and the depth of her pain led her to a devastating conclusion, one that she dared not speak aloud to anyone, not even to herself.

She had fallen in love with Cord. And that realization made her ache with despair, for she feared that there was no room for her in Cord Barrett's heart.

Twelve

Randee wiped the last drops of oatmeal from Rorey's face and lifted him out of his high chair. "Okay, sweetheart, what shall we do together on Mama's day off?" She balanced him on her hip for a moment as she wiped off the tray of his high chair. "We could go to the beach? Do you want to do that?"

Rorey merely grinned in response, and the sight brought an answering smile to her own lips. "Okay, that sounds good to me, too. You play with your truck for a minute while I rinse the dishes, then we'll get ready to go." Randee plopped the little boy down next to his current favorite toy and ran the water in the sink.

Randee was glad for the day off. The last week had been incredibly stressful. She still didn't know the source of the vandalism against her business, or if it would occur again. She hadn't noticed anything suspicious during the day on the boat, and after Kimo's surprise visit the first night, Cord's nighttime vigils had been uneventful. But in spite of that, Randee couldn't shake the feeling that whoever was behind the problems wasn't finished with her yet.

But that wasn't the only thing on her mind. The last week with Cord had been miserable. Each passing day seemed to underscore the helplessness of her situation. Their conversations had been limited to the necessary communication at work and nothing further.

The only exception had been yesterday. Cord had arrived for the afternoon sail exuberantly happy. He'd just come from the doctor, who'd told him that his leg had healed faster than anyone had expected and his walking cast could be taken off the next day. Randee had felt a rush of joy, not only because of Cord's good fortune, but especially because he was sharing it with her, and for the moment things were good between them.

Soon after, however, other feelings had intruded on her moment of happiness. She knew that as soon as Cord's cast was off, he would return to flying, and their relationship would once again be strictly a business one. Any chance of recapturing the intimacy that had seemed within their grasp only a week ago would evaporate.

Which was probably for the best. When she was being rational about it, Randee knew that the two of them had little in common on which to base a relationship; little, that was, except for an incredibly powerful physical attraction. For a while, she'd believed it was much more than that, but after the last few days, she wasn't so sure. Still, she couldn't forget how good it had felt to share the story of her marriage with him, to have someone who knew her secrets.

Randee finished loading the breakfast dishes into the dishwasher. She scooped up Rorey off the floor. "Mama will get dressed and get your bag packed and we'll head out to the beach." She was halfway down the hall to Rorey's bedroom when the doorbell rang. She glanced at her watch. Barely eight o'clock, awfully early for drop-in visitors. She went to the door and opened it, Rorey balanced on her hip.

Cord was standing there with the biggest smile she could ever remember seeing on his face. Randee stood for a moment in surprised silence.

"Good morning." His smile grew even bigger. "Are you going to ask me in?"

"Oh, Cord, good morning. I'm sorry, please, come in." She nervously passed a hand over her messy hair. "Sorry, I wasn't expecting to see you." Randee was suddenly conscious that she was still wearing the ragged, oversize T-shirt that she had slept in. What was he doing here?

"Rorey and I were just getting ready for a day at the beach. There's not some kind of problem with the boat, is there?" A sudden cold fear shot through her until Cord quickly reassured her.

Cord shook his head. "Nope, not at all. Don't worry about that. Everything's fine down there. That's not why I'm here." Cord continued to beam. A few seconds of silence passed awkwardly between them. Cord cleared his throat. "So, do you notice anything different?"

"What?" Randee was confused and flustered. "Notice anything different about what?"

"About me."

"Cord, I don't know what you're—" Randee suddenly realized that for the first time since she'd known him, Cord was standing on two perfectly good legs. "Cord, you got your cast off! That's wonderful! Congratulations!" Spontaneously, she hugged him and kissed him on the cheek. Rorey squealed, caught in the embrace.

"Whoa, better be careful. Don't want to squash the kid." Cord's eyes sparkled with a kind of simple, uncomplicated joy that Randee hadn't seen in him before. He extended his right leg and rotated it at the ankle. "Everything seems just as good as new. I'm a miracle of modern medicine."

"I'm so happy for you." In spite of her words, Randee could feel a dark pit forming in her stomach. She strove to remain cheerful. "So what are your plans? What are you doing on your first day back on two legs?"

"Actually, that's the reason that I'm here. I have a special surprise for you."

"What? What are you talking about?"

"You, my dear partner, will be spending the rest of the day with me on a secret adventure."

Randee felt her stomach drop with anticipation but forced herself to ignore the feeling. "Well, ah, Cord, that certainly sounds intriguing, but I can't go anywhere with you today. Today is Auntie Lani's day off, and I have to take care of Rorey." At that moment, Randee heard the familiar sound of three strong taps at the door followed by a key in the lock. "So you see there's no way that I can—"

"No problem." Lani closed the door behind her. "Cord and I already talk about it. Today's a special day for both of you." Lani took Rorey from her arms; she smiled at Cord, and her dark eyes had the spark of mischief that Randee had learned always meant that something was up.

"All right you two, what exactly is going on here?" She looked back and forth from Cord to Lani. "Cord?"

"You'll find out soon enough."

"Lani?"

Lani smiled an inscrutable smile. "I'm not telling you what to do, Randee, but if a gentleman was going to take me away for a special mysterious day, I think I would start by putting on some clothes."

Randee looked down at her tattered T-shirt and felt her cheeks flame. Lani patted Cord on the arm and gave him a conspiratorial wink. "You two have a good time. Come on, Rorey, let's get you ready to go to the beach with Auntie Lani." She carried the boy into his bedroom.

"Well?" Cord crossed his arms across his chest. "We're wasting time."

Randee held her breath as she searched for a snappy reply, but found none. She let out her held breath in a rush "Let me get dressed."

Cord kept his secret as long as possible. In spite of Randee's pleas, he would not offer her even a hint about where they were going or what he had planned. For most of the ride, Randee was baffled, but when they turned into the airport, she knew instantly what Cord's plan was.

"You are not taking me up in that thing!"

"That thing, as you so rudely call her, has been the source of my livelihood for the past ten years. I owe her a lot." Cord gestured affectionately toward the helicopter. "We've lasted longer than most marriages."

"How sweet. Then why don't the two of you go enjoy some time alone and I'll stay right here on the ground." Randee crossed her arms and slumped down in her seat. "I'm not going up in that thing."

"Come on, Randee. When Jason told me you'd never flown in a helicopter, not even once—"

"And I never will."

"I knew that was only because you'd never had the chance to fly with me."

"You're pretty sure of yourself, aren't you?"

"Only when I know I'm the best."

"Such modesty!"

"No modesty necessary. I'm the best helicopter pilot I know, period." Cord shifted in his seat. "Look, Randee, you don't have to come if you don't want to. I don't want to talk you into anything you don't want to do. But this is an important day for me, my first time back in the air in months, and I would really like for you to be there and see what this is all about." His eyes sparked with wry humor. "And after all, you do own fifty-one percent of this aircraft."

"Well, yes, but . . ."

"Why don't you just think of it as checking up on your investment."

"Okay." She was just being silly, she knew that. There was absolutely nothing to be afraid of, right? *Right. Just keep telling yourself that.*

Randee paced nervously as Cord quickly but carefully ran through the aircraft's preflight procedures. When he was finished he helped her into the copilot's seat and assumed the pilot's seat himself.

As Cord changed the settings on several of the mysterious instruments that covered the panel in front of them, Randee checked the buckle on her seat belt for the third time. The butterflies in her stomach were doing a tarantella. She decided to try one more attempt at an excuse.

"Speaking of my investment, isn't it a waste of fuel to be taking me sightseeing instead of paying passengers? That's no way for us to make money."

"My dear partner, you vastly underestimate me. I *am* making us money on this trip. You're just along for the ride."

Cord explained that they would be flying to the interior of the island to pick up a wealthy ranch owner and deliver him to the airport for a flight to the mainland. "We'll just take time for a little sight-seeing trip on the way."

"Well, in that case, okay. Expenditure approved."

Cord handed her a pair of earphones that would protect her ears and also permit them to communicate. Randee put them on, then entwined her fingers in her lap, kneading her own hands until they ached. The engine roared into life, and after a brief exchange with the control tower, they lifted off. *Lots of tourists do this every day,* she reminded herself sternly. *There's absolutely no reason to be scared.*

Randee felt the motion of the helicopter in her stomach, but within a few minutes of flight, all of her uneasiness was forgotten. Although she had spent most of her life in the Hawaiian Islands and thought that she was accustomed to the spectacular beauty that was their essence, Randee had never seen the splendor of the islands quite like this.

Cord began his flight heading north up the Kohala coast. Below them black lava fields stretched for miles to the edge of the sea, here and there stopping short of the water's edge to border a white crescent of sand and palm trees that had been spared the volcano's destruction. Each tiny beach was an isolated perfect paradise.

"Madame Pele's a powerful woman." Randee barely murmured the words, but the microphone on her headset carried them clearly to Cord's ears.

"You're right about that. And on the other side of the island she's still busy pouring out lava, making the Big Island bigger every day. Took out some more folks' homes while she was at it, too, not that long ago."

In what seemed like only a few minutes, they were rounding the upper tip of the island, passing over the town of Hawi. Cord turned the helicopter southeast, and the climate change was immediately apparent. Here along the Hamakua coast everything was lush and green with vegetation. Cord dropped down low enough for Randee to see the towering cliffs and deep valleys that the streams, winds, and surf had carved into the island. Back from the coast, green waves of sugarcane stretched as far as Randee could see.

"Pretty amazing, isn't it?" Cord's voice, even through the headset, conveyed a deep sense of awe.

"Yes, it is. Do you ever get used to it, seeing it this way every day?"

"Never. It's never the same from one day to the next; the island is always growing and changing. And yet, there is something ancient about it as well. Timeless."

The reverence in his voice drew Randee's attention from the spectacular sights below to Cord's face. In this moment, it was as if for the first time she could really see what was happening inside of him, see him with all barriers down. For some reason, the sensation moved her more than the incredible scenery they were flying over. Randee reached out and squeezed his hand.

"Thank you for showing me this."

"There's more, so much more." Cord smiled. "But duty, and money, calls, my dear partner." He began to turn the helicopter toward the island's interior. "It's time for me to pick up a paying passenger."

As they flew into the higher elevations, the weather began to change. The skies grew dark and threatening, and Randee could feel the outside temperature dropping rapidly.

"Are we almost there?" Randee tried to keep the worry out of her voice, but she could tell that Cord knew she was concerned.

"Relax, we're not far from Kiawe Ranch now. That's the Parker Ranch below us now."

Randee looked down at lush grasslands they were flying over, just a small section of the immense 225,000-acre Parker Ranch. Cord had told her that their destination, Kiawe Ranch, although a large ranch by any other standards, was nothing compared to the sweeping Parker Ranch. The Kiawe Ranch's owner, J. D. Perry, was a transplanted Texas oil baron and gentleman rancher who divided his time between the Big Island and his investments on the mainland. A tremendously energetic and impatient but good-hearted man, Perry had been using Cord's charter services for nearly eight years.

Rain began to splatter against the Plexiglas bubble that surrounded them, and a sudden burst of turbulence jerked Randee against her seat belt. Her stomach was beginning to churn, both from the motion of the flight and from fear.

"Cord, are we in trouble?"

"Don't worry. I can outrun this storm, no problem. We'll be at the ranch in plenty of time before the storm hits." He smiled, but Randee thought she could see lines of tension forming around his eyes. "Our biggest problem will be convincing Mr. Perry that we'll have to wait for things to clear up before we can take him to the airport."

Randee nodded, but she wondered if Cord was minimizing the situation for her sake. His cheerfulness seemed a bit forced, and she noticed a few beads of sweat were forming along his hairline.

Cord made some adjustments to the instruments on the panel in front of them. "Check your seat belt."

Randee tightened her seat belt, and at that moment the copter surged forward with a straining sound, then dropped back as if losing power. "Cord, what's going—"

The copter's engine made a sort of grinding sound, and the aircraft began to buck beneath them like an unbroken horse. Cord worked quickly, flipping switches on the instrument panel. The copter dropped again, and Randee screamed.

"Randee, baby, don't panic." Cord spoke without turning toward her, his full attention focused on keeping the helicopter steady. *That's right,* he told himself, *don't panic. She's doing fine. You're the one who needs to keep it together.*

Cord could feel his heart pounding, but when he spoke, he made sure his voice was steady and unhurried. "We've got some problem with the engine, so we're going to land. Luckily, we're in about the safest place we could be to make an emergency landing."

The copter bucked again. Cord's leg was throbbing with the memory of pain, memory that was uncomfortably recent. He gritted his teeth against the phantom sensation.

"We're going to be okay, so just close your eyes and hang on." *Right, buddy boy. You were telling yourself the same thing last time, right before you lost it, right before you went down. Some hotshot pilot you turned out to be.* Cord tried to tune out the mocking, whispering voices in his head, the voices that threatened to break his concentration and steal his control, but they kept coming back, louder and louder.

You can't do it. You're not going to be so lucky this time. And this time, you're taking someone else down with you. You're going to kill yourself and someone else, too. Not just anyone. Randee.

The Plexiglas dome was all silver now, nothing but sheets of opaque, silver rain. *Randee. You're killing Randee.* Cord dared to let his eyes flick toward Randee for an instant. But he didn't see the terror in her eyes that he expected; instead, she had her eyes closed, and her face was relaxed, in a gentle expression that could almost be called peaceful.

Like a bullet, the truth hit him. Randee was trusting him to save them. She believed he could do it. She believed in him. The thought banished the jeering voices in his head and collected his scattered thoughts back into order.

"Hold on, baby. I'm going to take care of you." This time, his voice was so soft, he might have been speaking only to himself.

Randee nodded, but she kept her eyes closed. She was thinking of Rorey. Cord was right. Of course they would be all right. She had to be. She had no choice; Rorey needed her. No matter what, she would survive.

Cord is in control, she repeated silently, *Cord is in control. He's going to take care of me.* The thought calmed her. She felt the helicopter descending, losing altitude rapidly in a fast, but controlled descent. The wind was buffeting the aircraft, but Cord was holding them steady. Randee kept her eyes shut, praying silently.

Seconds later, she felt the impact. Her body pitched strongly forward, her seat belt gouging into her abdomen and squeezing all breath from her, but she was held secure. It took her a few seconds to realize that they were firmly planted on the ground.

Randee opened her eyes, and as her vision cleared, Cord pulled her to him in a tight embrace. "We made it." At that moment, the storm struck with its full, awesome wrath. Rain pounded on the Plexiglass bubble with a deafening beat, and lightning split the sky, followed almost immediately by the deep boom of thunder.

"That lightning's close. Too close." Cord released his embrace but kept his hands on her shoulders. "Randee, we're going to have to make a run for it."

"What? What are you talking about? Can't we just wait out the storm in the copter?"

"No. The rotors may attract lightning. It's a slim chance but too dangerous to risk it."

"Where can we go? It looks like we're in the middle of nowhere."

Cord smiled grimly. "We are in the middle of nowhere, but I think we can find some shelter. When we were landing, I saw some kind of a building not too far from here, I'm not sure what it was, but it was probably less than two miles from here."

"Two miles!"

"Sorry, Randee, but there's no time to talk. This storm will be getting worse before it gets better. We need to get going."

Cord pulled an old windbreaker from behind his seat and wrapped it around her, then reached across her to pop open the door. When Randee stepped out of the helicopter's protection into the rain, she felt as if she had walked into her shower at home fully clothed. The windbreaker offered only meager protection, and within only a few seconds, she was drenched to the skin.

"Let's go. This way." Cord took her hand and they began to half run through the deep grass. At first Randee felt as if she were running underwater, unable to see anything but Cord beside her, leading her. Then for an instant, the landscape was illuminated by lightning, and all Randee could see was acre after acre of deep, green grasslands, dotted occasionally with a few scrubby trees. Then the dark of the storm descended again, narrowing her vision anew.

"Cord, how far is it?" Randee felt hot tears mixing with the rain, and she angrily swiped them away. She must not give in to her feelings. Too much was at stake. She didn't have the luxury of tears, not now.

"I told you, I'm not sure, but we sure as hell can't stay out here. Now just put your head down and hold onto me. We've got to move."

Randee grabbed Cord's arm and did as she was told, ducking her head against the sting of the rain. As she ran through the wet grass, she slipped several times, but Cord's arms were there supporting her, lifting her up. Each time he helped her get back to her feet and she would start again, forcing herself to keep up with Cord's pace.

They slogged on through the open fields. Randee felt as if they'd been running for hours, and after a while she no longer had any sense of what direction they were headed. In fact, she had begun to feel as if they'd been going in circles, covering the same stretch of muddy, rain-slicked ground over and over again.

The adrenaline rush that had started when the storm first began and that had carried Randee through the emergency landing and the beginning of their journey on foot was quickly fading. She felt tired and sleepy. Fatigue and numbness were invading both her body and her mind. Her legs felt heavy and clumsy beneath her.

She tripped again, this time falling face down in the grass. She got up on her hands and knees, then slipped back into the mud.

She tried to get up again, but this time she couldn't get her arms and legs to work right. She suddenly felt as if the mud was pulling at her, trying to suck her beneath its dark and slimy surface.

She tried to call for help, but no sound would come. But Cord seemed to hear her anyway, for his powerful arms scooped her up and pulled her tight to his chest. She tried to speak, to tell him that she only needed to catch her breath and she would be all right, to tell him not to worry about her, but before she could get the words out, everything went black.

Thirteen

Cord's back ached and his legs felt like lead. Water was streaming into his eyes, but he had no hand free to wipe it away. He paused for a moment, breathing deeply. He shifted the weight of Randee's body slightly to try to ease the throbbing pain in his back and strained to see through the dim afternoon. He searched for some landmark he recognized, anything that would orient him, that would give him a clue to their location.

Had he been wrong? They should have reached the building he'd spotted from the air by now. Maybe his sense of direction was off. Maybe he'd gotten turned around in the storm. There had been a stand of kiawe trees, he was sure of that, and not far to the north—

Lightning flashed, and with a flood of relief, he realized they were nearly there. The kiawe trees he'd sighted now stood just to his left about a hundred yards ahead, and just beyond and to the right was a small cabin. Cord pulled Randee tighter to him. She was limp and cold in his arms. "Hold on, baby," he muttered under his breath, "you'll be okay in just a few minutes." He headed toward the small structure.

As he'd hoped, the door was unlocked. There was no reason for security in a location as remote as this one. He pushed the door open and carefully maneuvered his burden through the door. Closing the door behind him against the torrential rain, he stayed in the doorway for a few moments, letting his eyes adjust to the dim light that filtered through the narrow, shuttered window.

The cabin was a single large room, apparently designed to be used as short-term shelter by a *paniolo* who might have to spend several days out tending to animals or repairing fences in this remote ranching area. The room was furnished sparsely but comfortably with a bed, a small table and two chairs, and a small sofa. Along one wall was a counter with a sink and a propane stove. In the opposite corner was a fireplace, an ample supply of wood neatly stacked beside it. A narrow door led to a tiny bathroom.

Once he could see, Cord put Randee gently down on the bed. He stood up and stretched the muscles in his back, listening to the rain drum on the corrugated metal roof.

"Cord? Cord, where are you?" Randee sat up straight, panic in her voice and her eyes shining bright with fear in the dim light of the cabin.

"Shh, everything's all right, I'm right here." He sat down beside her and put his arms around her. She held on tight to him. For a moment, she didn't speak, almost as if she was trying to determine if she was really awake or in the throes of some bizarre dream. Cord felt her body begin to shake, and he held on to her tighter.

"I was scared, Cord. I was so scared."

"I know. Everything's okay now." They stayed like that for a long moment, Randee seeming to absorb comfort from him, as if his mere physical presence was enough to make things right. Cord could have held her forever, just like that.

Finally she raised her head from his shoulder and looked around. "Where are we? What is this place?"

"Some kind of cabin. Probably only used at certain times of the year. Not exactly first-class accommodations, but at least it's fairly clean and, more important, dry."

"Ugh, which I'm not, and neither are you." Randee stood up and looked down at her dripping clothes. Pools of water were forming on the smooth floor. "Look at us! We've got to get out of these clothes." She was shivering uncontrollably. "I'm freezing."

"Tell you what. I'll start a fire, and you take a look in those two closets and see if there's anything dry we could change into."

While Randee searched the closets, Cord discovered matches and kindling in a wooden box near the fireplace, and soon he had a good-sized blaze going that shed a rich, golden light into the room.

The first closet that Randee inspected held some canned goods, a few candles, and little else, but to her relief, the second one did have some clothes hanging in it. She pulled out everything in order to see it better, and from the strange collection she found a man's T-shirt and a pair of shorts for herself; for Cord she found some dark blue sweatpants and an old flannel shirt.

Randee slipped into the bathroom and stripped off her wet clothes; her light cotton pants, blouse, bra, and panties were soaked. She tried on the clothes she'd found. The shorts were enormous, big enough for two of her, but they had a drawstring that she pulled tight around her waist, so they stayed up. The T-shirt was also big, but it was clean and dry, so she pulled it on gratefully. The soft, worn fabric felt good against her bare skin.

Randee emerged with her wet clothes in hand. "Your turn. I left some things for you in the bathroom." While Cord disappeared into the bathroom, Randee brought one of the folding chairs from the table near the fireplace and draped her wet clothes over it.

Cord came out of the bathroom, and Randee stifled a nervous laugh. The sweatpants were much too short, ending just below his knee, and the fabric was pulled tight over the heavy muscles of his thighs. The flannel shirt was too small to button across his chest, so he wore it open, exposing a broad stripe of bare skin.

"Hmm," Randee studied Cord's odd outfit, then looked down at her own. "We're both quite a sight. Maybe we'd better change shirts. This one might be better for you."

"Sure. Sounds like a good idea." Cord shrugged out of the flannel shirt, Randee's eyes following each movement. He stood waiting, shirt crumpled in one hand, wearing only the snug sweatpants that rode low on his lean hips. His feet and chest were bare, and golden tongues of light from the fire played over his body, highlighting his tawny skin. For a long moment they stood like that without speaking, eyes locked together. Finally, he extended the shirt to her.

"Here. You're welcome to it."

Cord's voice broke her from her reverie. Randee reached forward and snatched the flannel shirt from his hand and ran to the bathroom. She quickly changed, now conscious of the steady beating of her heart and her deep, ragged breathing. She returned with the T-shirt in hand.

"Now this might work better." She handed the shirt to Cord

and he pulled it on. The shirt was snug as a second skin, revealing every plane of his torso, but it did fit. "Yes, that's much better."

"That one's better for you, too." To Cord's amazement, even the worn flannel shirt was becoming to Randee, the wash-softened fabric draping softly over her full breasts. Her hair was already beginning to dry in the warmth of the cabin, curling slightly from the humidity where it swept her shoulders. Scrubbed clean of makeup, her cheeks were flushed with color and her eyes sparkled.

While they had been in danger, Cord had been focused exclusively on keeping Randee safe. That single concern had blocked out all other feelings. But now that they were okay and he had started to relax, his awareness of her as a woman had kicked into overdrive. Now that danger had passed, his body was vividly remembering the feel of her softness against him as he'd carried her through the rain; the feel of her pressed tightly against him, as even in unconsciousness she instinctively sought the warmth and protection of his maleness.

Cord turned away from her, suddenly painfully conscious of the swelling need of his body, which the thin fabric of the sweatpants did little to conceal. "Now, let's see what I can do about lunch." He started back to the pantry cupboard Randee had investigated earlier.

"Let me." Randee put a gentle hand on his arm, and the simple contact sent needles of sensation dancing over his skin. "You've been taking care of me long enough. You sit down by the fire and let me take care of this."

"Okay." Cord pulled a chair near the fire and watched Randee pad back and forth from the pantry to the counter. Watching her move, quick and graceful in her bare feet, only served to intensify his desire for her. Seeing her now, wearing ill-fitting clothes in this strange place, his mind leapt back to that first morning they had met, when she'd been dressed to the nines, all cool professionalism. She had been beautiful then, of course, there was no doubt about that. But now she was so much more.

There was something primal and basic about her now, an essential femininity that called out to him at a deep level, a level buried far below the civilized surface of his consciousness. She was warm, earthy, completely natural. And devastatingly sexy.

"Our choices are beans, beans, or beans."

"Hmm. How about beans?"

"Good choice." Randee lit the propane stove and searched for utensils. Before long the beans were warm. Cord thought he'd never smelled anything so delicious. Randee served them in chipped bowls she found in a cupboard over the counter.

"Not bad." Randee smiled at Cord from the chair she'd drawn near the fire. "Not exactly up to Auntie Lani's standards, but better than nothing." She took another bite. "And there's plenty more where these came from." She studied Cord's face. Gone were the small lines of tension that she'd seen so often around his mouth and eyes. He looked more relaxed than she could ever remember seeing him.

Thunder boomed in the distance, and the rain started to beat down with renewed vigor. "If this storm doesn't clear up, we may need all those cans. We could be stuck here for days." There was a husky quality to Cord's voice that sent a shiver all through her body.

"Days?" The thought caused the fluttery feeling in her stomach to intensify. "Well, I guess that's certainly one way of getting to know someone better. No TV, no books, not even Monopoly. Talking is about the only thing left to pass the time."

"You could say that." Cord's eyes were dark with an emotion that Randee was afraid to try to put a name to but that stirred a response deep within herself.

"Considering you're my partner, I really don't know very much about you at all, Cord." Randee took their empty bowls to the counter and returned to her seat by the fire. "You're something of a mystery."

"I'm hardly a mystery. There's really just not that much to know."

The afternoon had grown darker, and now virtually the only light in the room was from the fire. Emboldened by the darkness, Randee asked the question that had been on her mind. "If that's true, then we can start with the basics. Have you ever been married?"

"Yes."

It was difficult to read Cord's face in the flickering firelight, but his body language was perfectly clear: this was not a subject to be probed lightly. She waited for him to elaborate, but he did not. In spite of that, Randee was determined to press on. She'd seen Cord's shell begin to crack open the night Kimo had interrupted them on the *Kona Breeze*, and she desperately wanted to see if she could find another chink in that rough armor.

"How long ago was it?"

Cord looked up toward the ceiling, as if looking for the answer there. "Nearly ten years ago, now." He shook his head. "It was a big mistake."

"Who was she?"

There was silence again for a moment, and Randee wondered if she had gone too far, that she'd angered him. But maybe he'd only been gathering his thoughts, for when he spoke again, his voice was low and intimate.

"Her name was Brittany. I was crazy in love with her." His eyes were fixed on the fire now, and the flames' reflection shimmered back from them. "And maybe she loved me, too, in her own way. Or at least maybe she thought she did."

Cord paused and rocked back in his chair. "Her father was rich. Big-time rich. Owned a small resort on the Kohala coast, very private, very exclusive. Sort of a playground for the rich and famous. I used to pick up guests there sometimes for tours. That's how Brittany and I met. She'd just come home from college, flunked out actually, and Daddy was keeping her occupied around the resort. I guess she'd gotten pretty bored by the time I came along."

Cord smiled, a bitter, sardonic smile. "I suppose I was just the kind of distraction she'd been waiting for. Interesting, she called me. Nothing at all like the kind of soft little preppies she'd been used to. Not to mention that her father found me entirely unsuitable for his precious daughter, and that made me look even better to Brittany."

Randee waited in silence, hoping he would continue. After a moment, he did. "I should have seen the problem before things got serious between us, but all I could think about was Brittany. How lucky a bum like me was to get a classy girl like her. How I must've finally done something right. We got married right away."

There was silence for a moment, and Cord's voice dropped lower. "It didn't last long. I guess the novelty of being with somebody so daringly *inappropriate* as me wore off pretty quickly. But even more than that, Brittany liked nice things, and she was used to getting what she wanted. Daddy had always taken good care of her. I was working my butt off, but my business was never going to make enough money to satisfy her. Of course, as far as Brittany was concerned, there was a very simple solution to that."

"What?"

"She wanted me to give up flying and go to work for Daddy. Then I could make what she called 'real money.' " Cord snorted. "Can you believe it? The old man was even willing to give a lowlife like me a job, if that's what it took to make his little girl happy. Boy, I think she probably had her father wrapped around her little finger even tighter than she had me."

"Of course you didn't do it."

"I thought about it. I came damn close to doing what she wanted, throwing all my dreams away. I honestly did, because that's how crazy I was about her. But finally, I told her no, I just couldn't do it."

Cord dropped the front legs of his chair back onto the floor. "We had a hell of a fight, and not very long after that, she left me. I didn't even know where she was until I got the divorce papers two months after she was gone. I found out later she'd moved in with some doctor in Honolulu, a plastic surgeon, I think."

Randee was wise enough to know not to tell him how sorry she was for what had happened to him. He was not a man who would welcome anything that smelled of pity. But although she didn't show it, her heart ached for Cord, ached with the pain that he'd felt ten years ago and that was still a part of him now. Silently, she cursed Brittany, with words she'd never even spoken aloud in her life, for the hurt that selfish woman had inflicted on this man.

The rain beat heavier in a rhythmic pulse that reminded Randee of a heartbeat as the last dim light of the afternoon slipped away. The fire that had warmed them was now merely glowing embers.

Her own heart beating in time to the pulse of the rain, Randee slowly got to her feet and found the five votive candles she'd taken from the pantry cupboard earlier. She lit them and placed them around the room, moving silently through the darkness. Gradually, the room became filled with the delicate glow of candlelight, creating a dimly edged cocoon of gentle warmth and soft light.

When she was finished with the candles, she stood in front of Cord, waiting. He looked back at her, and his eyes were dark with yearning, with desire, desire for her alone, but he stayed where he was and made no move toward her. The sight of the desire in his eyes fanned the hot ache that Randee had been carrying within her all afternoon into a white-hot flame of need. She could wait no longer.

"I want you to kiss me." She heard the words before she realized she was speaking aloud. Now it was too late to take them back.

An agonizingly long minute passed before Cord answered her. She wanted his answer, *needed* his answer, now. When he finally spoke, his voice was dark and ragged, notes of warning and passion mixed in a dark blend that warmed her insides like strong brandy.

"If I kiss you, I won't be able to stop with that. Not now. Not this time."

Her answer came quickly.

"Then don't stop. Not this time."

Fourteen

Randee waited as Cord got to his feet, moving with an agonizing slowness that almost seemed designed to drive her mad with need. His eyes were locked onto her, holding her in place. She felt her breath come harder and faster in the long moments it took him to reach her. Finally, he was there, reaching for her, drawing her to him. She lifted her face to his, and he was there, his lips on hers, his mouth on hers.

The kiss was not gentle, not tentative. She had asked to be kissed, and she knew that Cord would give her what she asked for, what she needed. His right hand at the back of her neck told her that there was no turning back now, no stopping what she had so expressly set in motion. He kissed her slowly, deliberately, thoroughly, sending a message of possession that thrilled her deep in her belly. Without words, his kiss promised her that what was starting between them would not be finished until he had known all of her.

The heat of his mouth was working a strange, hot magic all over her body, and Randee suddenly knew she could not wait, she must have more, more of his mouth, more of his hands. Brazenly, she grabbed Cord's hand and placed it on her breast. At the first touch of his hand, her nipple pearled into a stiff peak, which he began to rub and tease with the broad pad of his thumb, stroking her through the soft flannel of her shirt even as his tongue continued its relentless exploration of her mouth.

Slowly, without breaking contact with her mouth, he began to unbutton her shirt, first the top button, then the next and next. Unable to stand the anticipation of his hands on her bare skin a moment longer, Randee took charge and unfastened the rest of the buttons herself, popping the last one off to skitter across the floor, in her eagerness to feel his touch. She gasped with pleasure as his rough palms first cupped both of her swelling breasts, then groaned into his mouth as his long fingers began to trace slow patterns over her puckering nipples. For untold minutes they stood like that, mouth on mouth, her breasts exploding with sensations that were radiating through her, down into her belly, down to her most intimate center.

When she thought she could no longer stand the exquisite agony of his hands on her, Cord bent down to take one hard peak into his mouth, Randee's head dropped back and a primal moan of pleasure escaped from her as he suckled and teased first one nipple, then the other, each kiss, each lick, each caress so very, very slow and deliberate Randee thought she might scream with the aching pressure of desire that was building within her.

Her hands, searching for an anchor in this sea of pleasure, found his rock-hard shoulders, and Randee began to knead the muscles there, straying to the back of his neck, then down his arms, then the back of his neck again, pulling his hungry mouth tight against her breast.

Her hands wandered down until she found the hem of his T-shirt, and she tugged it up to give her fingers access to Cord's skin. Greedily, she fingered the taut planes of his belly, his chest, searching, seeking, pleasuring, until Cord broke away with a groan to rip his shirt off over his head to remove any obstruction to her exploration.

And then they were finally skin-to-skin, her soft breasts pushed hungrily against his taut torso, the light dusting of coppery curls across his chest teasing her smooth skin.

Randee could feel the hard, thick ridge of his arousal trapped between them, pressed tight against her belly, and for an instant she pulled back, overcome with his size and power. But curiosity and desire won out, and a moment later she let her hand drift down and graze the front of his sweats, to brush him just slightly. Cord took in a breath between his teeth, a sharp sound of surprise and pleasure. Emboldened by his response, she kept her hand there and slowly let her fingers begin to explore him through the soft fabric, reveling in the growing ecstasy she could read in his face.

Cord let her have her own way with him for several exquisite minutes, her own excitement growing as she watched his breathing become deep and ragged and sweat bead across his brow. Finally, drunk with her power, she began to tug down the waistband of his sweats, anxious to feel him naked and heavy in her palm, but Cord captured her hand and brought it to his mouth.

"Stop. Not yet, love." He kissed her fingertips. "I can wait. Let me give you pleasure." He moved quickly to the bed and jerked the blankets from it. He spread them out in front of the dying fire. Without a word, he picked her up off her feet and gently laid her down on the improvised bed.

Again wordlessly, he knelt down and found the drawstring on her shorts and untied it. Seconds later, he had swept the fabric away, and Randee lay completely naked, the firelight playing across her glowing skin.

"You are so beautiful." Cord's gaze swept over her like a lingering touch. And for the first time in her life, Randee really felt beautiful; more than that, she felt voluptuous, sensual, desirable. She felt *cherished.*

Cord laid down beside her and kissed her, while he began a slow stroking of her body, a long, slow caress that started somewhere near her feet, played over her thighs, her hips, her breasts. Again and again he stroked her, his fingers pleasuring parts of her that she'd never considered even vaguely erotic, her calves, the back of her knees, her forearms; under Cord's searching hands her whole body seemed to have become one trembling mass of sensation.

But each stroke passed closer and closer to where she most wanted him without actually touching her there, until she was trembling with need. When his fingers finally brushed over the nest of dark curls between her thighs, she was nearly weeping for his touch and instinctively opened to him. She was hot and slick with arousal, and as he slipped two fingers into her, she dissolved into waves of shattering sensation. Now far beyond any conscious control, Randee felt her hips rolling and bucking, pressing hard against Cord's big hand with shameless abandon.

"Cord!" Randee cried out, lost in the swirling currents, but Cord drew her close into his arms, holding her tight against his solid body until the last waves of pleasure had abated.

Gently, protectively, Cord stroked Randee's hair, murmuring soft sounds of comfort, wordless reassurances. Although he was aching with need, heavier and thicker with desire than he could ever remember being, he was willing to wait. No matter how much he needed her, he would postpone his own fulfillment until she was ready for him.

Randee raised her head from his chest and smiled at him, a sleepy smile of contentment. Her eyes flickered over him, scanning his body, and he felt his swollen flesh jerk in response to her searching gaze. Her eyes met his, and without hesitation, Randee reached down and took hold of him through the fabric of his sweats. Her hand cupped him knowingly, possessively, sending an electric shock of sensation through him. Her voice was husky with the knowledge of pleasure. "Now. This time I want you inside me."

Cord stripped off the sweatpants and rolled on top of her, being careful to support himself on his arms so that his size and weight wouldn't hurt her. He stayed suspended over her for a long minute, savoring the final moments of anticipation before having what he had wanted for so long.

Randee opened to receive him, eagerly guiding him into her. Afraid of hurting her, he resisted the almost overpowering urge to plunge recklessly into her sweetness. Instead, he forced himself to enter her very slowly, being sure to allow her body enough time to stretch to accommodate him.

Concerned with her pleasure, his first strokes were careful, controlled, but when Randee cried out and grabbed his buttocks, urging him into her more deeply, matching him motion for motion, Cord felt his closely guarded control slip, and he was lost. Lost in the sweet sensations of Randee's body, lost in waves of desire and release that went far beyond any simple physical release he had ever known. Lost in the incredible feminine power this woman now wielded over him, and to which he was now so willingly in submission.

Randee's body shuddered beneath him, and the throaty sound of pleasure that escaped from her sent Cord careening over the final edge. His harsh cry of release blended with hers as he emptied himself deep into her, leaving behind the tight rein of control, finally daring to plunge willingly into the dark, unknown vortex that swirled far below.

Randee could not recall slipping into sleep, but she must have dozed, for when she opened her eyes the fire was only glowing ash, but she was not a bit cold. She and Cord were intimately entwined, arms and legs and torsos pressed as close together as was physically possible, and the combined heat of their two naked bodies had kept her surrounded with a delicious warmth.

Cord was asleep, and for several minutes she lay quietly, listening to the repetitive sound of the rain on the corrugated metal roof and watching the flickering patterns of candlelight move across the ceiling.

Cord stirred in his sleep, and Randee gave in to the temptation to gently stroke his cheek, now slightly darkened with dark blond stubble, half hoping that he might wake and make love to her again, half hoping he would stay asleep and leave her to her thoughts. Cord sighed deeply in his sleep and was quiet again.

What a contradiction this man was! Reckless, yet careful; somehow both wild and sensitive; rough, yet so tender. Randee took in a deep breath and let it out slowly. Her feelings were suddenly so clear.

She'd never felt like this about another man in her life. It wasn't just the lovemaking, even though he'd taken her to heights of sensation she'd never even dreamed existed. No, although her physical attraction to him was undeniable, it was much more than that.

When she'd fallen in love with Max, she'd been falling in love with an image, a picture, a lie. In the end, she'd had to accept the bitter fact that she'd never really known her husband. But now with Cord, Randee was discovering more about who this man really was every day.

The closer Cord let her get to him, the more he let her see who he really was beneath his sometimes thorny exterior, the more she cared for him. Yet she knew how dear he held his privacy, how closely he guarded his personal world; a world that for many years he'd occupied alone. There was no guarantee that he would ever feel comfortable sharing that world with her.

He'd been deeply hurt. Now that Randee knew the source of his pain, the reason for his withdrawal into that private world that admitted no visitors, she knew that she had little reason for hope. After Brittany's duplicity, after she had used him and his love and then discarded him, Randee could understand why he'd given up on people, given up on caring for others, and letting others care for him.

Just as she herself almost had. Just as the lies of J. Maxwell Turner had threatened to cut her off from ever loving again. But she had never been alone, for she had Rorey, and she'd poured all the love she had, all the love that Max had rejected, into loving her son. Maybe that was why, in spite of the pain and hurt she'd suffered, she'd never dried up inside, never stopped believing that love was still real, that love was still possible.

And now she loved Cord Barrett. And no matter what might happen in the future, for this night, in this private haven away from the rest of the world and its responsibilities, that one fact would have to be enough.

"Hey. You're awake." Cord's eyes were still at half-mast, heavy with interrupted sleep, but there was no mistaking the desire that was there, and as he let his gaze wander over her naked body, Randee could feel her skin warm and glow from his simple attention.

"Yes, for the last few minutes." She snuggled closer to him and laid her palm flat against his stomach, fingers splayed wide over tan skin. She drummed them up and down lightly on the taut muscle. "I've been listening to the storm. But I haven't heard any more thunder."

Cord cocked his head, listening. "Yeah, but the rain still sounds pretty heavy." He began to kiss the skin just below her left ear, very slowly and deliberately, sending a shiver through her body. "Can't really tell much until morning." He reached for her breast, palming it with an easy familiarity. "So, do you want me to start the fire again?" His thumb flicked over her nipple in a rough caress.

"I—I don't think—" Her body was already responding to his touch, as if her senses had all been turned up to a heightened level. "I—" Suddenly she seemed to be having difficulty speaking. Her nipple peaked, aching for his tongue.

"What?"

"I don't think we need the fire." She guided his mouth down to the spot where her flesh burned for it.

"Good. I don't think so either."

She was already wet, and this time he slipped into her easily, sheathing himself to the hilt in one stroke. Randee made a moaning sound of pleasure, and Cord captured the sound, covering her mouth with his and kissing her hard before whispering heavily in her ear. "I've got all the heat I need right here."

Fifteen

Randee opened her eyes and stared at the unfamiliar ceiling, completely disoriented. Where was she? She tossed back the worn blue blanket that had been tucked around her and sat up, panicked. After a moment of confusion, she recognized the cabin, which was now bathed in a strange steel-colored light. The door was standing open, and Cord was silhouetted against the gray light of the morning, looking out toward the fields.

He turned around and smiled at her, steaming coffee cup in hand. "Good morning." He was dressed in his own clothes from yesterday. A damp breeze blew in the door, and Randee suddenly realized she was sitting naked on the floor amid a jumble of blankets. She made a grab for the blue blanket and covered herself before she answered.

"Good morning." When she moved, she became aware of a slight soreness throughout her body, not at all unpleasant, but a vivid reminder all the same of the intimacies of the night before. The sensation immediately brought back a flood of images from last night, images that almost glowed in her mind with the patina of polished koa wood.

"So, ah, how's the weather?" Randee almost laughed at the banality of her question, especially under these strange and intimate circumstances.

"Rain stopped sometime early this morning." He glanced up at the sky. "We've still got some pretty heavy cloud cover, but it looks like things are on the move up there." He closed the door and smiled, but Randee thought she saw a trace of regret in his face. "So it probably won't be too long before we can get out of here."

"Great." Randee wasn't nearly as enthusiastic as she was trying to sound. As strange as this whole experience had been, she wasn't ready to leave behind this little cocoon that had sheltered them from the storm and been warmed by their lovemaking.

"Do you want coffee? I found some instant."

"Umm, sure." Cord turned to the pan of steaming water on the propane stove, and Randee took advantage of the moment to find her dry clothes. In spite of last night, she felt strangely modest in front of Cord. The boldness that had empowered her last night seemed to have evaporated.

"I'm afraid there's no sugar, or milk, or anything. We're lucky to have the coffee." When he turned back with her coffee, she was buttoning her blouse.

"Did everything dry okay?" Cord's eyes regarded her with an intimacy that sent a ripple of memory through her body.

"Fine." She bent to brush some dried mud from the knee of her pants. "I'm grubby, but dry." She straightened up and took the coffee from him.

"Me, too. Do you want to take a look outside?"

"Sure." Randee followed him outside. The sky was rapidly clearing, and patches of blue sky were appearing here and there. As far as she could see, their cabin was the only structure in sight, a tiny island in a sea of billowing grassland broken only by occasional stands of kiawe trees and a distant fence line. "Wow. We really are in the middle of nowhere. Where's the helicopter?"

"About two miles that way, I figure, just beyond the second rise."

"Only two miles? It seemed a whole lot farther than that yesterday."

"You can say that again." He playfully arched an eyebrow in her direction. "Of course, that all depends on the method of transportation."

She put her hand on his arm. "Oh, Cord, I'm sorry. After everything that happened, I never even thanked you for taking care of me yesterday!"

He shrugged. "You aren't that heavy."

"That doesn't matter. I should have been able to take care of myself. I don't want to be one of those helpless female types."

Cord put his hands on her shoulders and looked into her eyes, not speaking. Finally he smiled. "Baby, that's about the most ridiculous statement I've ever heard. You're the strongest woman I've ever met." He leaned down and kissed her gently, and Randee felt warmth begin to radiate through her. Just as she had last night, she was daring to let herself believe that Cord really did think she was special, that he cared for her in a different way.

The sun broke through the clouds, and Cord gently ended their kiss. "Well, I guess we ought to go see how the copter fared in the storm." He kissed her again quickly. "Time to pack your bags, lady. It's checkout time at this charming little inn."

Randee rinsed their coffee cups and returned the blankets to the bed they'd never used. Watching her carefully make up the bed, Cord laughed.

"I didn't know you were a neat freak. I suppose next you'll be looking for the vacuum cleaner."

"I'm not a 'neat freak,' as you put it." She fluffed the single pillow and put it carefully back in its place. "I just believe in being a good guest."

"Good idea." Cord retrieved the borrowed clothes from the floor where they'd dropped them last night and put them back in the closet. "After all, we do want to be invited back for another visit."

Randee met him in the middle of the room, standing close to him without touching. "Do we?" She searched his face for meaning. "Want to be invited back, I mean?"

"Damn right we do." He cupped her chin in one big hand and tipped her face up to meet his. He kissed her again, this time long and hard, and Randee felt desire begin to stir within her. Her passion rose to match his, and she pressed her body tight against his. She could feel him against her, already fully aroused and ready. An unfamiliar sense of pride in her womanhood filled her as she realized the powerful effect that she had on Cord.

She led him to the narrow bed, both of them shedding clothes as they moved, until they were completely naked by the time they reached the bed. This time their lovemaking was quick, filled with an intense need that each strove to fill in the other. Unlike last night, where in the dim light of candles Randee felt as if time had been suspended, now in the morning's growing brightness she was overwhelmed with the sensation of time running out.

That sensation seemed to overwhelm their lovemaking, and so it seemed exactly right that this time the peak came high and soon. Afterward, they lay together in silence for a few minutes, holding and caressing, communicating without speech, each seeming reluctant to break the silence of the morning. Finally Cord spoke.

"Randee."

"Mmm."

"Randee, I sure don't want to, but we really do have to get going. Some folks are going to be awfully worried about us by now."

"Oh, no." Randee sat up suddenly. "Rorey! Auntie Lani! What was I thinking? They must be scared to death!" She got up and scrambled into her clothes, overwhelmed with guilt. "Cord, we've got to get back! I can't believe I've been so irresponsible! What was I thinking?"

"Irresponsible? Randee, slow down." Cord captured her in his arms. "In case you've forgotten, we didn't plan any of this. It's not like we stole away for the weekend. And up until about an hour ago, there was no way we could leave, so don't make yourself sick feeling guilty. Okay?"

"Okay. I guess you're right. But please, let's hurry. I want to go home."

The hike back to the helicopter was muddy but fairly easy. The copter had settled rather unevenly into the soft, wet grass but otherwise looked normal. Randee stood by nervously as Cord carefully inspected the aircraft, looking for any damage that might have happened during their forced landing. He circled the copter slowly, then climbed inside to take a look at the instruments in the cockpit. After a few minutes of flipping switches and checking gauges, he climbed back out and walked around the copter one more time. Finally he stepped back and dusted off his hands.

"Well?"

"Believe it or not, it looks like we managed to take this bird down without a scratch. The wet grass gave us a pretty soft landing. The radio's not working, but that's about all I can find so far."

"That's great! Can we get going?"

Cord shook his head. "I'm afraid not. You're forgetting that what got us here in the first place wasn't the storm at all, it was the engine trouble. I can't find anything wrong, but I don't want to take it up until Jason's had a chance to check everything out."

"But how are we going to get home?"

"We'll have to head for the highway. It shouldn't be more than another six miles."

"Six miles!" Randee's feet already ached. The thought of more walking was unbearable.

"Then we can flag down a passing car and hitch a ride into Kamuela—" Cord stopped and squinted into the distance. "Well, maybe not. It looks like we're in luck."

"What? What do you mean?" Randee tried to follow the line of his gaze.

"Looks like the cavalry has arrived."

Two men on horseback appeared over the gentle rise, coming from the same direction she and Cord had earlier.

"Paniolos. I feel like I should be in some old Western movie." Randee had seen pictures of the Hawaiian cowboys before, but never face-to-face. She knew that even with modern technology, such men were still essential to the Big Island's ranches.

The two men reined up their horses. "Cord!" A middle-aged, bandy-legged man dismounted his horse and grabbed Cord's hand with both of his. *"He aha ka pilikia?"* He nodded toward the helicopter.

Cord clapped the man on the shoulder. "I don't know what the trouble is yet, Neki, not exactly, but I'm going to find out. I'm awfully glad to see you. We were just getting ready for a long hike. So how far are we from Mr. Perry's place?"

"You're at the very eastern edge of Kiawe Ranch, Cord. You almost made it. When you didn't show up last night before the storm, Mr. Perry got very worried. He sent me and Philipo out to search for you this morning as soon as it was light. So what happened?"

Cord explained quickly about the engine trouble and the forced landing. "We took cover from the storm in the cabin south of here."

Neki looked at Randee and gave Cord a significant glance. "Thank goodness that at least you were not lost by yourself." A broad smile crinkled his leathery face, and he lifted his hat to Randee in a gallant gesture of greeting.

"Neki, how far are we from the main house?"

"Not far by horse. If you'll just lift your lady friend up behind me, I'm sure Philipo won't mind sharing his horse with you."

J. D. Perry, a rangy middle-aged man in a battered cowboy hat, welcomed them effusively, glad to see they were safe. "Cord, my friend, am I glad to see you! I was afraid Neki and the rest of the boys might be finding pieces of you all over the ranch this morning."

"Not this time, Mr. Perry, not this time." Cord put his hand on Randee's shoulder. "This is my partner, Randee Turner." To Randee's tremendous surprise, Mr. Perry took off his cowboy hat and swept low in a gallant bow.

"Prettiest partner I've ever seen. You're a lucky man, Cord." Randee felt herself grow red and was momentarily at a loss for a reply. Luckily, Cord jumped in with the story of the storm and the emergency landing.

"But I'm awfully sorry I made you miss your flight, Mr. Perry. I know you're a busy man."

"Don't worry about it, Cord. Life's an inch long, my friend." He spread his thumb and forefinger in illustration. "So there's no time to lose sleep over what can't be helped. Besides, as I've told you before, where other men see problems, I see opportunities."

J. D. Perry pushed his stained hat far back on his head and grinned. "So this particular *opportunity* gives me an excuse to call up my good friend Tony and tell him I'm tired of always having to meet on his turf. If he wants to do business, he can damn well just come to me this time." J. D. Perry leaned over to Randee with a conspiratorial wink. "Gotta keep straight who's the boss in these situations, isn't that right, my dear?"

They declined Mr. Perry's offer of breakfast, saying they had to get back home as soon as possible. Mr. Perry offered them the use of one of his Jeeps for the trip back to Keauhou Bay. Cord and Randee gratefully accepted. But before they left the ranch, they called Auntie Lani and Jason to let them know they were okay.

Randee buckled herself into the passenger seat of the Jeep as Cord started the engine. She waved goodbye to Mr. Perry, then settled back against the comfortable seat. "Whew. We're finally on our way home." She wondered why the thought made her feel so unsettled.

Cord nodded. "Finally." They followed the twisting gravel road out toward the gate of Kiawe Ranch, onto the main highway. Randee felt the silence between them grow awkward. Finally, Cord spoke again.

"You should have heard Jason on the phone. You wouldn't have recognized old Mr. Calm and Collected."

"He was pretty upset about the copter, huh?"

Cord chuckled. "I would say so. Let's just say I heard some words I didn't think that boy even knew."

"Does he feel responsible?"

"That's putting it mildly. You know he does all the maintenance on it himself, doesn't trust anybody else to do it right. He swears everything should be in perfect condition. He's driving up here today to check everything out. He's probably already on his way."

"I'm sure, whatever it is, he'll figure it out."

Randee put her head back on the seat, suddenly weary. It was already noon, and as they descended from the mountains, the temperature was rising. She felt dirty and sore, and she desperately need a long, cool shower. A dull headache was beginning to throb above her right temple.

"We should make it back to Keauhou Bay by two o'clock. I wonder how many passengers we had on the morning cruise."

Randee merely shrugged in response. Cord's attempts at conversation were leaving her cold. Where were the words of tenderness, of caring that he had spoken last night and early this morning? Perhaps what she'd thought was honest sharing of their feelings was simply talk. Perhaps she had been a fool to think that was anything more than the afterglow of their physical union.

Randee felt as if she were reentering real life after a long trip into some kind of fantasy world, a world that was reduced in size to only one room, one room and two people. A world that had been devoid of real problems and responsibilities. A world in which Cord had awakened feelings within her she hadn't known existed. A world that would be impossible to recapture. A world that she was better off trying to forget she had ever visited. A sadness she did not fully understand was stealing over her.

Cord studied Randee's face surreptitiously, trying to read her thoughts. A lot had happened between them in the last twenty-four hours. Even now, dirty and tired, she was still the most desirable

woman he'd ever seen. She'd faced a terrifying situation with re-
markable courage. She was like no other woman he'd ever met,
and she affected him like no other. He put his hand on her knee.

"So, do you think you'll ever be brave enough to try this
again?"

"Try what again, Cord?" She lowered her head back against
the headrest and closed her eyes.

"Flying with me." Cord let his hand move up her thigh a few
inches. "And all the rest."

Randee opened her eyes. She covered Cord's hand with her
own and squeezed it tight. She looked unsure, as if she were
searching for just the right words, and when she finally spoke,
her voice was carefully modulated, friendly but somehow also
distant.

"Cord, right now I'm so tired I really don't know what to
think."

"Come on now, you're not getting off that easily," he said, at-
tempting to force a light tone onto the conversation. "You still
didn't answer the question."

He heard her take a deep breath before answering. "Well, I
have to admit it, at the moment, the idea of flying does sound
pretty scary to me."

Randee met his eyes for a moment, then leaned her head back
again. "I think I'll try to get some sleep before we get back to
Keauhou. I've got a lot of work to do this afternoon." Randee
shut her eyes tight, and Cord slowly withdrew his hand from her
grasp.

He felt as if she'd thrown a bucket of ice water in his face. To
him, the message was clear. He was good enough for a quick
tumble, a low-class thrill, as long as no one else was around to
see. But he'd better think again if he thought she was going to
let him into her life. Just like Brittany, she'd tire of him soon
enough.

Cord hit the accelerator and passed the slow-moving truck in
front of him. He edged the speedometer up to eighty, his gut
aching. No matter how fast he drove, it was still going to be a
long way home.

Sixteen

Cord parked the Jeep in the lot above Keauhou Bay and shut off the engine. He looked out over the bay. Aboard the *Kona Breeze*, he could see Kimo and the crew preparing the boat for its afternoon trip. Randee was still asleep in the seat next to him. She had slept most of the way, and during the long, silent drive his anguish had gradually subsided to a dull, familiar ache that felt like an open wound in the middle of his chest.

He should have been smarter, he knew that now. Hell, from the beginning he'd tried to keep his distance, tried to let the memory of Brittany keep him from letting things get out of hand. But that hadn't been enough. In spite of all the warning bells going off in his head, he'd plunged ahead. And now, the very thing he'd sworn could never happen, *must* never happen, had come to pass. But this time, it was worse than Brittany. Far, far worse.

Randee stirred and opened her eyes. "We're home?" She sat up straight and looked around.

"Yes, we're home." Cord opened his door and hopped out of the Jeep. "We're in time for the afternoon cruise." He slammed the door. Randee was still a bit disoriented from her nap in the Jeep. Why was Cord being so abrupt?

Randee caught up with him as he reached the dock. "Cord, is there something wrong?" Before Cord answered, Kimo left the boat and hurried up the dock to meet them.

"Randee! Cord! Thank God you're here." Kimo threw his arms around Randee and hugged her, something he'd never done before. "What a long night it was! Jason called me and told me what happened. It has been a time of great worry, but thank God at least you two are okay." Although he was smiling, Kimo's normally happy face was lined with concern. He appeared to still be quite anxious about something.

"Yes, we're safe, Kimo. But you've known that for hours. Is there something else bothering you? Has something happened to the boat?" Randee braced herself for more bad news.

"No, no, don't be frightened, the boat is fine. Nothing like that. Nothing for you to be concerned about."

"Kimo, if something's bothering you, I want to know what it is."

"It's nothing, Randee, I'm sure. It's just that—well, Liko is missing."

"Your son?" Cord's voice came out of nowhere. He seemed to be tuning in to the conversation from some faraway place. Randee suppressed her annoyance.

"Missing? Kimo, what do you mean?"

"Yesterday he was supposed to help me with some painting on the boat in the late afternoon, after everything was cleaned up from the last trip, but he never showed up. I was angry, but I wasn't at all worried, but then he missed dinner, too. I waited up till midnight, but then he never came home at all!"

"Maybe he is staying with friends and just forgot to mention it to you."

"I called his friends, the ones I know anyway, his old friends. No one has seen him since yesterday morning. I'm just worried sick, Randee. I've had some trouble with Liko over the past few months, a couple of terrible fights, but nothing like this! He's never just disappeared!"

"Kimo, I know you're upset, but I'm sure wherever he is, Liko's okay. After all, he's a grown man."

"Eighteen, yes, and big, too. But not a man, not yet, I am afraid. Not in his mind. Not in his heart." Kimo shook his head and walked back down the dock toward the boat, his shoulders sagging.

"I think I'd better help Kimo finish getting the boat ready." Cord followed Kimo without a backward glance toward Randee.

The afternoon trip was fully booked, and two of the crew had called in sick, so in spite of her fatigue, Randee had to come along to help out. Cord came too, although she hadn't asked him, and Randee was especially grateful that he was there since Kimo was preoccupied with Liko's disappearance and needed a lot of help.

The trip passed quickly, and there was never a moment when she and Cord were alone together. A heavy curtain of awkwardness had descended between the two of them, and after the intimacies they'd shared, it seemed especially bitter. The time they'd shared in the cabin already seemed a distant memory, or even a dream.

They returned to Keauhou Bay and assisted the passengers off the boat. Randee sent Kimo home early to get some rest; it was obvious the poor man's mind was elsewhere. She and Cord would stay and supervise the cleanup crew. By the time they were finished, it was nearly dark. Since Randee's car was still at the airport where she'd left it yesterday morning, Cord drove her home.

Cord turned the ignition off and let the Jeep's engine die. The overhead light in Randee's carport came on. "Well," he cleared his throat, searching for something to say to cover this awkward moment. "You're finally home at last." He tried to smile at Randee, but even he could feel the strain in it. What was she thinking right now? Did she regret everything that had happened between them?

The door opened with a bang and Auntie Lani emerged, Rorey in her arms.

"Randee!"

"Mama!"

Randee bolted from the car, door swinging behind her. "Oh, my baby, my boy, let me kiss you." Randee took Rorey into her arms and hugged him tight. "Did you miss me? I sure missed you." The intensity of her embrace for Rorey, the obvious depth of her love for the little boy touched Cord deep inside. He felt a stab of something strangely like envy. What it must be to be loved like that.

"From what Jason told me, the two of you had some real adventures." Auntie Lani clucked with maternal concern and laid a chubby hand on Cord's arm. "I thought I would go crazy with worry. Kimo came over in the evening and sat with me as long as he could, thank goodness. We were both so frightened." She dabbed at her eyes. "I am so glad to see you safe! Ah, you both must be starving. I made a special dinner."

Cord looked over at Randee, trying to gauge her response. He didn't know where he stood with her now. She'd been pleasant, no, *civil* was more like it, while they were aboard the boat this afternoon, but little more, and she'd seemed to have wanted to avoid being alone with him.

"Ah, thanks Auntie Lani, but I don't want to be any trouble. I should be—"

"Nonsense, Cord, it's no trouble. There's plenty to eat, even for a big man like you. You must stay." She turned to Randee. "Isn't that right, Randee?"

Cord held his breath, waiting for her response.

"Well, I think—" The insistent ring of the telephone interrupted her. "I'd better get that." Randee disappeared into the house.

"Come on in, Cord." Lani took his arm and gently pulled him into the house. "You just sit down and let Auntie Lani find you a cold beer."

"What?" Randee juggled Rorey into a better position and put the phone closer to her ear, praying she had misunderstood what she'd just been told. "What did you say?"

Jason's voice was calm, the way Randee was used to hearing it, but tonight there was an undercurrent of tension beneath the calm that crackled over the phone line. She'd never heard it in him before.

"I said, I checked out the copter very carefully, and it looks like the damage was deliberate."

"What do you mean by 'deliberate'?" Randee heard her voice shaking. Auntie Lani, sensing some trouble, took Rorey from her arms.

"I mean the copter was sabotaged. The gas tank's got all kinds of crap in it. Not a very sophisticated trick, but plenty effective."

"Cord." Her voice was a small squeak, a tiny appeal for help. She held the phone away from her like it was some dangerous object she was anxious to be rid of. "Cord, please." Without another word she handed the phone to Cord.

Randee sank down on a chair, barely aware of the brief, pithy dialogue that followed between Cord and Jason. She was jerked from her daze when Cord slammed down the phone, biting off a vicious curse she'd never heard from his lips before.

"Cord, what does this all mean?" She was trembling, and more than anything right now, Randee wanted him to take her in his arms, tell her everything would be all right; to comfort her as he had during the storm.

"It only can mean one damn thing. Whoever tried to kill us by spiking the copter—"

"Kill us?" Randee felt as if she might pass out. "That's crazy! Why would anyone want to kill us? Oh my God, Cord, do you really think—"

"Of course I do. There's no other explanation. Why the hell else would anyone do a thing like that? Whoever the bastards are, they've got to have something to do with all the other crap that's been happening on the boat." Cord's eyes flamed with anger and menace. "And I've got a damn strong hunch that after this last stunt, they're not going to stop now." Cord was now pacing the room, no longer able to contain the energy of his fury.

Rorey started to fuss and whine softly, acutely aware in his intuitive toddler's way of the taut wire of anxiety that ran between the adults in the room. Auntie Lani quietly disappeared down the hall with him, patting his back gently and whispering soft words of comfort that did not betray the worry in her dark eyes.

"I'm going down there." Cord stopped his pacing and moved quickly toward the door.

"Where? What are you talking about?"

"I'm going to stay on the boat tonight." As Cord spoke the words, an overwhelming sensation of apprehension swept over Randee.

"No! Cord, you can't, it's too dangerous. I can't let you take that risk."

"Randee, there's no point in arguing about it." He was already at the door. "I'm going."

"Then I'm going with you."

"Don't be ridiculous. You said yourself it's too dangerous. You're staying here. I can take care of myself. I don't have time to take care of you." His eyes were flinty with determination. "The last thing I need is you tagging along and getting in the way."

"I don't want you there alone."

"Look, Jason is already on his way back from the ranch. I'll leave a message for him at his place to meet me at the boat when he gets home."

"That won't be for at least another two hours."

"I told you, I can take care of myself."

"It's my boat, and I'm going with you."

"Randee, listen to me—"

"Damn it, Cord Barrett! You listen to me!" She grabbed his arm in a vise grip of determination, her fingers digging deep into the muscle. "I love you! Maybe nobody else gives a damn if you get yourself killed, but I do, and you can't stop me from caring!"

The words hit Cord like a sharp blow to the stomach, knocking the air from him, making it nearly impossible for him to speak. "Randee, don't—I—I—" The fire in her eyes burned the words from him. Finally, he simply said, "All right, then. Let's get going."

Never had a silence seemed so thick, thought Randee, as thick as the dense vapor that poured forth from the seething Kilauea caldron. The ride back to Keauhou Bay seemed to last an eternity, while her mind raced back and forth from the danger to her business, to Cord, and to herself. For she had exposed herself now, she knew that. There was no going back now. But she knew she'd had no other choice. The words had almost spoken themselves.

By the time Cord pulled into the parking lot, Randee's imagination was running on overdrive. She almost expected to see the boat missing, or half swamped, or engulfed in flames. After what she'd been through, no disaster would surprise her.

But instead of destruction or disaster, the *Kona Breeze* floated peacefully at the dock, secured by her lines, looking just as she had any other evening Randee had been here late working in the office, as if to make a mockery of her fears. And yet, even so, something still wasn't quite right.

"Randee, I want you to stay in the Jeep, just until I check things—"

"No." Randee had no intention of obeying and didn't wait to hear more. She opened her door and hopped out. It was too late now. She'd come this far, she wasn't going to let him go now. "Don't bother arguing. I'm coming with you."

Cord gave her a look she couldn't interpret, but he closed his door without comment. He started toward the dock. "Then stay behind me."

Randee nodded and let Cord lead the way, but she stayed close behind him. The normal appearance of the boat had not calmed her imagination, and her heart was pounding strongly. The dock creaked beneath her feet, and she jumped back with a gasp. Cord whirled around.

"What? What is it?"

"Nothing." She brushed her hair out of her eyes and willed her heart to slow its wild beating. "I—I'm sorry, I guess I'm a little jumpy."

He put his arms around her but did not draw her to him. "That's all right. You're not the only one." His hands on her felt as if they were there to restrain her, not to comfort her. "Listen, Randee, everything looks okay. Now you've seen it for yourself. So why don't you take the Jeep and go home, okay? Jason should be here before long."

"No." In spite of her nervousness, Randee's voice came out strong. "I'm not leaving you here."

"Randee, this isn't some little adventure we're on here. This isn't the movies." Cord's mouth was set in a hard line of disdain that sent a chill over her skin, in spite of the balmy night air. "This is not a game. This is for real. Just go home where you belong."

"Damn it, Cord, stop it! Stop it right now! I'm not her, damn it!" The words were out of her mouth before she knew it.

"What are you talking about?" His voice was low and icy with some dark emotion. Randee took a deep breath. There was no going back, not now. The wound was deep and ugly and inflamed by the infection of the years, but she forced herself to probe it.

"Brittany. I'm talking about Brittany, Cord."

"Let's just leave her out of this."

"No, Cord, I'm not. I'm not going to leave her out of this, because she's still here. She's right here with us, as real as if she were standing here between us." Cord's eyes were flashing with barely leashed emotion, but Randee could not stop now.

"I know she hurt you, Cord. She took your love and made a mockery of it." Randee felt hot tears spilling down her cheeks. She dashed them away with the back of her hand, damning her own weakness. "You trusted her, and she humiliated you. And ten years later you're still hurting and angry. Cord, if you hate her now, I don't blame you one bit. She deserves it. My God, sometimes I even think that I hate her, too, because of what she did to you."

A moment of silence hung between them. Cord's face looked as if it were carved of stone.

"But I'm not Brittany. And I don't deserve your anger, or your condescension, or your bitterness." Randee forced what little control she had left onto her shaking voice. "I haven't hurt you, or betrayed you, or used you. Frankly, the only thing that I'm guilty of is loving you. Maybe that shouldn't have happened. But it's too late now."

"Is it?"

"Yes. You're not getting rid of me, Cord Barrett. Not now." Randee waited as the long silence grew between them. Finally, Cord spoke.

"I'm sorry, Randee. You're right, you're not Brittany, and you don't deserve to be treated like her. I'm sorry for being such a jerk."

"Apology accepted." Randee waited, hoping for more, some insight into his feelings for her. She'd laid herself bare, and for what?

To her surprise, he didn't speak, but instead encircled her in his arms and drew her body against his. He held her tight against him, and to her surprise, Randee thought she felt the solid length of his body trembling against her. After what could have been hours but was probably only one or two minutes, he broke their embrace. He put one hand under her chin and tipped her face up toward his. He looked into her eyes and kissed her only once. "I guess we'd better check out the boat."

Cord stepped onto the boat, then turned and offered her a hand. They stood for a minute on the open stern, hands together, the only sound the water lapping gently against the hull. Cord dropped her hand and walked down the two steps into the dark interior of the lower cabin. Randee followed close behind, and slammed into Cord's back when he stopped suddenly.

"Cord, what are you—" Randee suddenly saw what had stopped Cord. Directly to their right was the door leading down to the engine compartment. A pale light was bleeding from underneath the door.

Cord pushed Randee back against the port wall of the cabin with a forceful shove, turning back just as the light snapped off and the door to the engine compartment swung open. A tall figure emerged from the compartment and Cord dove for him, knocking both of them down to the floor of the cabin.

"Cord!" Randee's breath had been knocked out of her, and she was plastered tight against the wall of the cabin, unable to distinguish in the shadows who Cord was struggling against. Randee tasted blood in her mouth, aware in some distant corner of her mind that she had bit her lip. Her eyes strained to see through the darkness, searching to see what was happening. She wanted desperately to help Cord but was paralyzed by fear and darkness.

The two men rolled to the far side of the cabin, and in the dim light Randee saw the intruder stand for a moment before Cord grabbed his leg and pulled him back to the ground. There was a scraping sound, Cord's voice, strong in the dark. "Randee! Lights!"

Frantically, Randee searched for the switches near the steps. She scraped her hands against the rough fiberglass as she desperately sought the banks of switches. After what seemed an eternity of searching, she finally found them and flipped them on. The overhead lights came on, bathing the scene in a harsh white glare.

Cord held the intruder pinned to the deck, a knee in his back holding him down and his right arm twisted around behind him. The intruder's face was smashed tight against the deck, but he was turned toward Randee, and distorted as they were, she could make out his features.

"Liko! What are you doing here?"

Liko growled like some caged animal, then spat out a string of vile curses, all directed at Randee. She felt her stomach seize with fear and revulsion at the undiluted hatred that was spewing forth.

Cord shoved Liko's face into the deck. "Answer the lady's question, scum. What are you doing here?"

"It's all your fault! All of it!" Liko's words were twisted with rage, and even though Cord had him subdued, Randee stepped back with fear.

"Liko, I don't understand. What are you talking about?"

"You stupid bitch! You brought it on yourself! You stole the

Kona Breeze from my father, and now we have nothing! Nothing, do you understand?"

Liko's rage now abruptly seemed to transform into some other emotion, and suddenly he was crying and sobbing, then keening like some wounded animal. In that horrible instant, Randee realized that Liko was not rational, he was drunk, or high, or even insane.

Cord grabbed a fistful of Liko's hair and lifted his head a few inches from the deck "So tell us, you miserable scum. Did you sabotage my copter?"

"Yes! And you both should have died in it!" Liko spat out the words with something strangely like pride. "And the boat, too. I did it all, all by myself. She deserved it, all and more, the stupid, selfish bitch!"

With a surge of unnatural strength, Liko made a break from Cord's grasp. Cord was thrown to his back, and Liko stood and kicked him viciously in his weakened leg. Cursing in pain, Cord again dove for Liko, struggling to pull him back down to the deck.

"Cord! Oh my God!" Randee screamed, fear tearing at her heart like knives. At that moment a new large presence jumped down the steps into the fight. Randee screamed again, then recognized the new figure. "Jason!"

Liko turned in surprise, and Jason landed one solid roundhouse punch to his jaw, just as Cord dove for Liko's knees. Liko buckled and hit the deck with a sobbing, bubbling cry of pain and rage. Seconds later, Liko was again securely pinned to the deck, this time under the substantial weight and strength of Jason Clay.

Cord got to his feet, wavering a bit unsteadily and bleeding from his mouth and nose, but his voice was strong, even a little arrogant.

"Go up to the office and call the cops, Randee, and stay up there until they come." He wiped the blood from his mouth, and even managed to give her a small, tight smile. "And tell them they'd better hurry, because I don't know exactly how long little old Jason and I can keep this crazy bastard down without hurting him."

Seventeen

"I'll never be able to forgive myself." Unshed tears shone in Kimo's eyes, and his big hands gripped the back of his captain's chair, the pressure turning the skin over his knuckles white. "And I know you won't, either." Kimo lowered his head, unable to meet Randee's eyes.

The morning sail had been canceled to permit the police to conduct their investigation aboard the *Kona Breeze*, and Randee, Cord, and Jason had each given their official statements regarding the bizarre events of the night before. After taking dozens of photographs of the boat and asking what seemed to Randee nearly a hundred questions, the police had finally finished their business and Jason had left to supervise the repairs to the helicopter.

Now, before she and Cord had even had a minute alone together to sort out what had happened to them in the last two days, Kimo had shown up to tell Randee he was resigning from his job. Randee thought she had never seen a sadder sight than the big man trying to make sense of the strange events of the last twenty-four hours.

"Kimo, you mustn't blame yourself. Cord and I both know you're not responsible for what happened." Randee looked to Cord for verification. Cord was leaning against the lifelines, a large bandage on his temple and several scrapes on his arms and legs, but otherwise none the worse after his encounter with Liko. Cord shrugged noncommittally.

"No, Randee. I am responsible. There is no question in my mind about that." Kimo's dark eyes were filled with pain. "I should have known, I should have recognized what was happening with my own son. That was my duty as a father." Kimo shook his head sadly.

"I still don't understand what Liko meant when he said I stole the *Kona Breeze* from you. Do you?"

Kimo nodded. "I'm afraid I do. You know I worked for Mr. Haster for many years, nearly twenty years now." Randee nodded. "Well, a few years ago, Mr. Haster promised me that when the time came for him to retire, he would sell me the business. He said he would give me a good price and help me get a loan to buy him out. He told me that was to be his way of rewarding me for all the years of my life I'd given to him and the *Kona Breeze*." Kimo's eyes were distant with memory. "Liko and I used to talk about it quite a lot when he was younger, and dream about what we'd do when the *Kona Breeze* was our very own. Every evening we'd talk about it."

"But it didn't work out that way, did it?" Randee prompted. She tried to keep her voice gentle, but she wanted to hear the whole truth.

"No, of course it did not. That man, that Mr. J. Maxwell Turner—I am sorry, Randee, but I never trusted that man, not for a minute—he came along and made Mr. Haster a very big offer; the whole deal had something to do with some waterfront land that Mr. Haster owned, that was the whole reason for it. That J. Maxwell Turner had no interest in the *Kona Breeze*, never! But in any case, it was an offer I could never hope to match." Kimo looked down at his hands for a moment. "So Mr. Haster took J. Maxwell Turner's offer. Told me he was sorry, but business was business."

"How did you feel about that?"

"Naturally, I was angry!" Kimo looked up, a bit of his old spark returning. "I was very disappointed that Mr. Haster hadn't kept his promise to me. But I understood that he wanted to get the best price he could for the business, and so eventually I got over it. But Randee, I certainly never blamed you for anything that happened!"

"But Liko did?" Cord was at Randee's side now, as if she needed protection.

"No, not at first, I don't think. In fact, I thought Liko had lost all interest in the boat; he never wanted to come to help out, never. Not like before! This past year, we've grown so far apart; we fight all the time! And the fights, they are always the same. Always over money. No matter how much I gave him it was never enough." There was a long, painful pause. "And now I know why."

"Cocaine?" Cord's voice was like a knife, all sharp, cold steel. Randee sucked in her breath, feeling how the word hurt Kimo, but said nothing.

"Yes. That's what they've told me." Kimo lowered his head, the shame almost too much for him to bear. "Cocaine, and another poison they call crystal meth. That's where all the money was going." Kimo swiped at his eyes, fighting the tears that were threatening to overwhelm him. "And I never suspected, not ever." Kimo swallowed hard several times before he could continue. Randee waited in silence, knowing he would finish when he was ready.

"The drugs ruined his mind, Randee. Destroyed him. Gave him crazy ideas. He had got it in his head that there would always be plenty of money for him if the *Kona Breeze* were mine, and then, of course, he assumed that the business would eventually belong to him. Somehow, he felt entitled to all of that." Kimo took another deep breath and paused for a moment. When he spoke again, his voice was a bit steadier. "But you see, Liko believed that money was somehow the real problem, not the drugs."

Kimo walked to the lifelines, looking out toward the ocean as if he might not ever see it again. He stood that way for a few moments, then turned back to Randee and Cord. "So please, forgive a foolish father for not seeing this sickness in his own son." Kimo walked to the stairs, head down. He stopped before starting to descend. "Good luck, Randee. Good luck, Cord." His voice broke. "I'll miss you both and the *Kona Breeze*." He started down the steps.

Cord watched Kimo, sorry for the man, but understanding his choice. Hell, he'd quit, too, if he were in the same situation. There would be no choice, after what had happened. A man had to live with his mistakes, no matter how painful; no matter what it cost him. God knows he always had.

"Kimo, wait." Randee went after him, catching him halfway down the steps. She put a hand on Kimo's arm. "Please come back for a minute." She led him back up to the deck as if he were a child. "Look, Kimo, I know how hard this must be for you. But honestly, the mistakes that Liko has made have nothing to do with you. Liko has a drug problem, Kimo; it's an addiction, a sickness, and he needs help. Your job is to see that he gets it." She steered Kimo back to the captain's chair. "But this is where you belong, Kimo, right here in this seat. I want you to stay."

"But Randee—"

"The *Kona Breeze* would never be the same without you. Please don't quit, Kimo. We need you here."

"Randee, do you really mean it?"

"Of course I do."

Kimo turned toward Cord. Hope was lighting his face, but he was still nervously twisting his hands together.

"Cord, what do you think? It's important what you think as well. I mean you're the one that Liko . . ." He gestured toward Cord's bandaged head.

Cord hesitated until he saw the look in Randee's eyes, a look that left no doubt what answer she expected from him. He let out his breath in a heavy sigh of resignation. "Oh, hell, Kimo. It's just a scratch. Besides, my partner there makes all the decisions anyway."

"Please, Kimo? Will you stay?"

"Yes, Randee!" Kimo threw his arms around Randee. "Thank you! I can never repay you for this. I must go visit Liko, but I'll be back in time for the afternoon trip!" Seconds later, Kimo was down the ladder and running down the dock like a much younger man.

"You've just made someone very happy." Cord watched Kimo drive away, waving ecstatically from the window of his truck. Kimo honked cheerfully and disappeared up the road.

Cord turned back to Randee. "You're quite something, partner."

Randee shrugged. "Well, if I let Kimo slip away, not only would I have to find a new captain, but I have a hunch that Auntie Lani would be pretty upset with me, too, if you know what I mean." She cocked an eyebrow and smiled at him, and Cord felt the warmth flooding from her eyes into him, warming him inside. "I think that maybe she's got her own plans for Kimo. What do you think?"

"I think you may be right about that."

"Besides," she shrugged again, "it was just the right thing to do."

"You seem to have a knack for knowing the right thing to do."

Somehow, Randee could always forgive, really forgive, not just say the words. Her capacity to care for other people in spite of their flaws was humbling. He'd never experienced anything like it. She could even care for someone like him. Cord felt something cracking open within him, some final hardness dropping away from his heart.

And last night she'd said she loved him, said it right out loud. He'd been afraid to hear the words, afraid of the magnitude of what she was saying. But she hadn't been afraid to say them. Could he find that courage as well?

Cord took her hand and led her to the front of the deck, looking out toward the mouth of Keauhou Bay. "Do you remember the first time we stood here?"

"How could I forget? That was the same day we signed the partnership agreement."

"I'm glad you mentioned that subject. That's something we really need to talk about."

Randee's heart began to beat faster. "What did you have in mind?"

"I think we need some changes in our partnership agreement. I'd like to renegotiate." Cord put his arms around her waist, drawing her close to him.

Hope was growing within Randee. "Well, that would all depend."

"Depend on what?" Cord was nuzzling below her ear now.

"On what terms are being offered." She gently pushed Cord back so she could look him in the eye. "Let me hear the terms, then I'll decide."

"Randee, I'm not an easy man to be with, I'd have to be the first to admit it. And I've been alone a long time. Till you came along, the only one who could tolerate me was my dog." His eyes crinkled in a smile. "And I'm afraid that even she was getting a little tired of me."

Randee smiled back, but his smile quickly faded into seriousness. "All I've got to show after living on this island for the last fifteen years is my business, and you already own fifty-one percent of that. But for what it's worth, I'm willing to give you the rest."

"The rest of your business?" Randee wrinkled her nose quizzically.

"I mean the rest of me. I love you, Randee. I want to be a whole lot more than your business partner." He gently framed her face with his hands, his eyes locked onto hers. "I want to be your husband. I want to be a father to Rorey." With incredible tenderness he pushed back a lock of her hair that the morning breeze was toying with. "I don't want to live alone anymore, and I don't want to live without you anymore. So what do you say? Will you have me?"

Randee drew him to her and let her kiss give him the answer first, a long, deep union that neither wanted to end. Finally, she broke their kiss.

"Yes, Cord. I'll have you. I love you."

"Does that mean we now have a new partnership agreement?"

"Yes, I'll take the new terms. But this time, there's not going to be a fifty-one/forty-nine percent split. This time around, each of us is going to get a hundred percent."

COMING NEXT MONTH

Plus four other great romances!

AVAILABLE THIS MONTH: